Rafe

Also From Sawyer Bennett

Arizona Vengeance Series
Bishop
Erik
Legend
Dax
Tacker
Dominik
Wylde *(coming 5/12/2020)*

Jameson Force Security Series
Code Name: Genesis
Code Name: Sentinel
Code Name: Heist
Code Name: Hacker
Code Name: Ghost *(coming 6/30/2020)*

Wicked Horse Vegas Series
Wicked Favor
Wicked Wish
Wicked Envy
Wicked Choice
Wicked Wedding
Wicked Knight
Wicked Angel
Wicked Secret *(coming 5/26/2020)*

Cold Fury Hockey Series
Alex
Garrett
Zack
Ryker
Hawke
Max
Roman
Lucas

Van
Reed
Marek

Sugar Bowl Series
Sugar Daddy
Sugar Rush
Sugar Free

Love Hurts Series
Sex in the Sticks
Jilted

Wicked Horse Series
Wicked Fall
Wicked Lust
Wicked Need
Wicked Ride
Wicked Bond

Off Series
Off Sides
Off Limits
Off the Record
Off Course
Off Chance
Off Season
Off Duty

Last Call Series
On the Rocks
Make It a Double
Sugar on the Edge
With a Twist
Shaken Not Stirred

Legal Affairs Series
Legal Affairs
Confessions of a Litigation God

Friction
Clash
Grind
Yield
Sexy Lies and Rock & Roll
The Pecker Briefs

Standalone Books
The Hard Truth About Sunshine
If I Return
Uncivilized
Love: Uncivilized
Finding Kyle
Atticus

Rafe

An Arizona Vengeance Novella

By Sawyer Bennett

1001 DARK NIGHTS
PRESS

Rafe: An Arizona Vengeance Novella
By Sawyer Bennett
Copyright 2020
ISBN: 978-1-970077-99-5

Published by 1001 Dark Nights Press, an imprint of Evil Eye Concepts, Incorporated

Sign up for the 1001 Dark Nights Newsletter
and be entered to win a Tiffany Key necklace.

There's a contest every month!

Go to www.1001DarkNights.com to subscribe.

**As a bonus, all subscribers can download
FIVE FREE exclusive books!**

One Thousand and One Dark Nights

Once upon a time, in the future…

*I was a student fascinated with stories and learning.
I studied philosophy, poetry, history, the occult, and
the art and science of love and magic. I had a vast
library at my father's home and collected thousands
of volumes of fantastic tales.*

*I learned all about ancient races and bygone
times. About myths and legends and dreams of all
people through the millennium. And the more I read
the stronger my imagination grew until I discovered
that I was able to travel into the stories... to actually
become part of them.*

*I wish I could say that I listened to my teacher
and respected my gift, as I ought to have. If I had, I
would not be telling you this tale now.
But I was foolhardy and confused, showing off
with bravery.*

*One afternoon, curious about the myth of the
Arabian Nights, I traveled back to ancient Persia to
see for myself if it was true that every day Shahryar
(Persian: شهريار, "king") married a new virgin, and then
sent yesterday's wife to be beheaded. It was written
and I had read that by the time he met Scheherazade,
the vizier's daughter, he'd killed one thousand
women.*

Something went wrong with my efforts. I arrived in the midst of the story and somehow exchanged places with Scheherazade – a phenomena that had never occurred before and that still to this day, I cannot explain.

Now I am trapped in that ancient past. I have taken on Scheherazade's life and the only way I can protect myself and stay alive is to do what she did to protect herself and stay alive.

Every night the King calls for me and listens as I spin tales. And when the evening ends and dawn breaks, I stop at a point that leaves him breathless and yearning for more. And so the King spares my life for one more day, so that he might hear the rest of my dark tale.

As soon as I finish a story... I begin a new one... like the one that you, dear reader, have before you now.

Chapter 1

Rafe

Raleigh, North Carolina—the City of Oaks. I'm home, and this homecoming sucks.

This is where I was born and raised, but right now, I have no sense of welcome. Instead, with a sense of dread, I traverse the airport terminal with the other passengers who just deplaned the direct flight from Phoenix.

Four days ago, I was a member of the Arizona Vengeance hockey team and scored the game-winning goal against the L.A. Demons to secure our number one playoff spot. Life was great.

Three days ago, my father called me with the devastating news that he had pancreatic cancer and was dying. He had weeks left, at most.

Two days ago, I asked Dominik Carlson—owner of the Arizona Vengeance—to trade me, release me...whatever. Just let me get back home to Raleigh to be by my dad's side for as long as he had left.

One day ago, I said goodbye to my team. My brothers. My hockey family.

Today, I'm home, and I'm not ready for any of this.

I'm sure it's inconceivable to many that I would ask to leave the Vengeance when they are poised to make history as the first expansion team to have the talent and depth to win a Cup championship. But not one of my teammates made me feel a fool for my decision. They all stood by me in solidarity and support. Dominik—as he insists everyone call him—pulled magical strings with the Cold Fury management and almost overnight, I had a new team.

With that news, I realized I was going to my hometown of Raleigh, North Carolina, to play—and watch my father die at the same time.

Yesterday, I attended a party at Dominik's home. Even though I was officially off the roster, I still felt very much a part of the Vengeance family. Still do, for that matter, even though I'm officially a member of the Carolina Cold Fury now. Those bonds won't be broken so easily, but I truly understand that my loyalty is now with my new team. I'm sure new bonds will form.

I know it may still be up for debate in Vegas and among sports experts, but in my heart, I know I've left behind a team that has an indescribable magic to their unity. It's something I'll probably never see again in my career, and that makes me sad. It's a sense of loss I'm trying to process, right along with the one I'm about to suffer soon with my dad.

So here I am, stepping foot onto the small escalator heading upward that will deposit me outside the secure portion of the terminal and at the foot of another escalator that descends right back down to baggage claim. I packed a large suitcase full of clothes and essentials to get me through until the movers can get here with my stuff next week.

As I locate the correct baggage carousel, I realize I'm not in a good mood. I'm absolutely furious at this change in life circumstances. Not angry at what I'm leaving behind, but what I'm walking toward. A life where I get to watch my father die, something I'm woefully unprepared for.

I don't even really know how to feel about it. My father, Jim, and I haven't always had a good relationship. Growing up, I found him to be cold and distant, a hard man to know. He's an electrician and, in my childhood, worked long, hard hours to provide for his family. He would come home at night and expect my stay-at-home mom to have dinner on the table.

After dinner, he'd retire to his recliner and watch TV for the rest of the night, and I had to be quiet and not disturb him. It was my mom who helped me with homework, made sure I was appropriately bathed and put to bed at night. She's the one who woke me up in the morning, fed me, and waited with me at the bus stop.

Only after I showed some natural talent for hockey did my dad's interest in me perk a bit. I mean...he came to some of my games when his work schedule allowed, and while he was never one to boisterously cheer me on, I could tell he was proud. It was the look on his face.

Still, it was Mom who dutifully brought me to every game and nursed my sprains and injuries. When I doubted myself, she always bolstered me back up. She's the one who encouraged me to keep pushing day in and day out to develop my talent.

And she's the one who held back her tears so I wouldn't feel guilty when I left to live with my billet family in Green Bay to play Junior A hockey at the age of sixteen. She knew it was my best chance to move forward in my path to play professional hockey, even if it meant giving up the last two years of my childhood and being with her full-time.

It's true... I grew a little closer to my dad after I entered the professional hockey league, but that had more to do with the fact that I was an adult, and thus we had more things in common. While the bond with my mother has always been exceptionally tight and emotional, my relationship with Dad has been more like that of the proud uncle who lives down the street. We've never had the in-depth discussions one might imagine occur between father and son, and he's never been the one I turned to for guidance and support.

And yet, when he called me to tell me he was diagnosed with cancer, it stunned me that it was actually him delivering the news. Based on our history, I would have considered it normal for him to have my mom pass on the bad news, but I heard something in his voice then that I'd never heard before.

Thinking about it now, it's hard to describe, but if I have to boil it down to one word, it might be something close to regret.

Not that he's dying, but perhaps that we missed out on far too many things together.

Whatever it was I heard in that conversation, it was enough for me to ask for a trade to the Cold Fury. Although I don't have a deep relationship with my father, it was enough for me to walk away from an assured championship, and possibly set my entire career back.

The baggage carousel alarm starts to blare, and then the gears kick in, starting the platform in its three-hundred-and-sixty-degree journey to deliver luggage. It jolts me out of my thoughts, and my gaze moves to the little ramp that leads up from the bowels of the airport, where some worker will be carelessly chucking our bags.

The various pieces start their climb upward and dump unceremoniously out onto the metal platform that will eventually deliver the items.

I move closer to the carousel, finding an open spot between

passengers. Flying first class has its perks, one of which is that my bag has a priority tag. It comes out third in line, and I nab it easily.

My mom is supposed to pick me up and is probably waiting out by the curb. I set the heavy suitcase on its wheels, pull the telescoping handle up, and turn toward the door, immediately knocking into someone because I'm not watching where I'm going.

"Shit," I mutter, my hand automatically extending to steady the person. "I'm so sorry."

My gaze travels up past jeans-clad legs, a pretty spring sweater in butter yellow, gorgeous breasts, and a slender neck.

Then my eyes lock on the most beautiful face I've ever seen.

One I've looked at least a million times throughout my life and in my dreams. I still have found none to rival it. My entire body jolts with an electric shock as I stare into the eyes of my ex-girlfriend, Calliope Ramirez.

"Hey," I say in mild surprise, both pleased and feeling terribly awkward at seeing her here. I look around for her family or even some friends she might be on a trip with. When my gaze comes back to her, I ask, "Small world, running into you at the airport."

Could that be any lamer?

I mean...we grew up together. Our houses still sit side by side. I've known her for as long as I can remember, and it's a pure miracle that she and I haven't run into each other since we broke up eight years ago.

But no...this is the first time I've laid eyes on her in a very, very long time, and damn if she hasn't gotten even more beautiful over the years.

Calliope is my age...twenty-six. Our birthdays are only ten days apart. We celebrated all of them together, seeing as how we were the best of friends growing up and then way more later.

I take every bit of her in. Her long, dark hair parted in the middle and cascading in loose waves over her shoulders. Her skin a light mocha, compliments of her Puerto Rican dad, but the rest of her face is classic Irish from her redheaded mom. Her eyes are hazel-green, more on the green side when she's feeling intense emotions, and she has a smattering of freckles all over her nose and cheeks. She's got the Irish temper to boot.

"Your mom sent me to pick you up," she replies flatly, her eyes conveying that she's not overjoyed to see me. "Your dad's having a bad day, and she didn't want to leave him."

In that moment, I forget all about my sad history with Calliope. The way I broke her heart and left her behind for fame and fortune. At least, I'm sure that would be her story if you asked her to tell it.

"What do you mean by *bad day*?" I ask her, my heart thudding in my chest.

For just a moment, her expression softens in empathy, and she gives a small shake of her head. "I only meant that he's really tired, and your mom doesn't like leaving his side hardly at all. I've been pitching in when I can to help out. She asked me to come, so I came."

"Okay," I reply, gusting out a relieved exhale of air. I attempt a smile. "Thank you for doing that."

"Sure," she replies with a shrug and turns on her heel toward the exit doors. I scramble to catch up with her, pulling my suitcase along.

Wordlessly, we head out of the airport into the parking garage and take an elevator up to the fourth floor. I follow Calliope to a later-model Nissan Pathfinder that, although clean, bears a few rust spots near the fender. I notice a parking decal for Raleigh Community Hospital and of course, I know that Calliope is a nurse.

I actually know quite a bit about her because, over the years, I've never been hesitant to ask my mom how she's doing. I do it because I'm riddled with so much guilt and regret over what I did to her all those years ago that I have to torture myself with all the details of her life that don't include me.

So, yeah... I know she's a labor and delivery nurse at the local hospital, and while she doesn't live with her parents anymore, she still lives close by and visits them frequently, so she still sees my mom quite a bit.

Because Mom still thinks I'm the world's biggest idiot for leaving Calliope behind, she tends to overshare details about her.

Including information I'd rather not know, like the men she's dated over the years.

Bitterness fills the back of my throat because leaving Calliope behind was truly the biggest mistake I've ever made. At the time, I thought it was best for her, and I sacrificed my own happiness to give her the best shot at life I could.

It's painful to see her now, just like it's going to be painful to see my dad before too long.

Yeah...this homecoming sucks.

I'm silent for several minutes as Calliope navigates her way out of the airport terminal and heads onto the beltline that circles Raleigh. We grew up on the southeast side of the city, not in the best area, but not in the worst either. Definitely blue-collar and lower middle class. Calliope's dad is a mechanic, and her mom is a music teacher. It's funny but I remember being slightly jealous of Calliope growing up. Her dad had a trade profession, the same as mine. Owned his own business, same as mine. Yet her father always seemed to be more involved in her life than my dad was in mine. I knew that while my mom always made excuses for my dad's physical and emotional absence, blaming it on the stress of his job and owning a business, it really couldn't be all that true since Calliope's dad was very present in her life.

"So, how are things going with you, Poppy?" I ask her, hating the silent void that actually hurts my ears, particularly since her radio is off. I'm a bit shocked how easily I slipped into calling her by her nickname that I'd given her when we were younger, but I press forward. "I understand you work as a labor and delivery nurse?"

Calliope's neck twists as she briefly takes her eyes off the road to give me a sour look. "Look, Rafe... I'm sorry about your dad and what you're going through right now. I'm sorry you had to come home to this, and I'm actually really committed to helping your parents get through it because I care for them deeply. So you might see me around from time to time. But that doesn't mean you get to know anything about my life or how I'm doing. It's off-limits to you, okay?"

I grimace and turn my gaze out the passenger window. "Yeah...got it."

"Good," she snaps, and I sneak a glance back her way. She's gripping the wheel so tightly her knuckles are turning white. I knew she'd probably have hard feelings, but I guess I didn't think she'd still be this bitter after all these years.

I should leave well enough alone, but I have other things driving me than merely wanting to reconnect in some way to this beautiful creature I left years ago. "Do you mind talking to me about my dad?" I ask her quietly.

Calliope jerks, her head snapping my way, eyes round with surprise. "Excuse me?"

"My dad," I prompt. "It would help to have maybe a bit more perspective as to what I'm walking into."

"What do you want to know?" she asks cautiously.

I take a deep breath, the bazillion questions, fears, and insecurities I have about my father's cancer overwhelming me. I try to focus. "He told me on the phone he doesn't have long...maybe just weeks, but he didn't give me details. And I tried to talk to Mom about it, but she just cries when I ask, so I left it alone. I don't want her more upset than she already is. I need information because I'm feeling a little lost and out of control right now."

I watch Calliope carefully, and while she doesn't look my away again, her expression is soft with sympathy as she gives it to me straight. "It was just too advanced by the time he went to the doctor. He's been sick for a long time but kept putting it off, always needing to work. You know how your dad is."

I nod because if there's one thing I know, it's where I got my intense work ethic from. He worked all the time, long hours, and we rarely took vacations. I can even remember him working on major holidays like Christmas and Easter. He certainly missed a good chunk of my games growing up because of work.

"He's going to decline pretty rapidly," she says, and the tone of her voice is different. This isn't pretty, sweet Calliope Ramirez talking, but a seasoned and educated nurse who may not deal with cancer in her line of work, but clearly knows something of which she speaks. "Your parents have already decided to use hospice to come in once he needs more skilled care, but for now, he's still able to ambulate, eat, and take care of basic life-care skills like dressing himself. He's just really tired a lot now. That will be the biggest thing you'll notice."

A lump settles in the base of my throat, and I can't even speak past it. She must sense it's not enough information for me to truly understand what I'm facing, so she continues.

"As his body fights the cancer, his organs will start to shut down. He won't be hungry, so he won't want to take in nutrition, and that will further weaken him. He'll eventually become bedridden. At some point, he'll go in and out of consciousness."

My biggest fear—the thing I've been obsessing about—pushes forth, past the constriction in my throat. "Will he be in pain?"

"No," she replies quickly and with such assurance, I believe her. "The great thing about hospice is that they will prescribe medications to make him incredibly comfortable. He won't feel pain at all."

The rush of breath that escapes me is guttural, but it leaves a hollow pit in my stomach. He won't feel pain, but he'll be unconscious and heavily sedated when he dies. That should make me feel better, except for the fact that he's going to die, and there's not a damn thing I can do about it.

I feel the absurd need to cry, which I refuse to do. It's not something I can afford to give in to, and I think I'd rather die myself than let Calliope see me at my lowest.

"Thanks," I manage to say, completely grateful for the information she's provided and yet, a small part of me hating I had to rely on her for it.

She doesn't respond, but the silence doesn't feel so heavy anymore. My worst fear—my father dying in pain—has been alleviated. Now I can start to process the rest of it.

Of course, I'll have to fit that in among other things like finding a place to live—eventually—and joining my new hockey team. Lots to do, and little time to do it in.

I already feel so very tired, and it's only just begun.

"Hey," Calliope says, her voice a mere whisper, but it shocks me to my core that she's initiating communication.

My neck twists, and I give her my regard, my expression unassuming.

"I'm glad to help you navigate through the medical part of it," she tells me, sparing a glance my way so our eyes lock. "I promised your mom I would help out when I can...as things progress. If you can't talk about stuff with them, you can ask me, okay?"

The gesture is appreciated, especially since I know she doesn't want anything to do with me. It's really not surprising, though. Even though Calliope must hate me for dumping her, she's still the kindest person I know. It's why she's a nurse. She loves helping people and easing their pain, whether it be physical or the type that's lodged deep in the soul.

I merely nod my gratitude at her and turn my attention back to the window, starting to mentally prepare myself for my reunion with my dying father.

Chapter 2

Calliope

Gritting my teeth, I stew over the unfairness of everything. Jim is dying from pancreatic cancer, his wife Brenda is falling apart, and now Rafe has returned home to witness it all.

Damn it all to hell, that man.

What I can't figure out is why I feel so freaking angry. It's not like I obsess about Rafe and what he did to me all those years ago. In fact, I manage to go days—sometimes an entire week—without thinking about him at all.

But it's hard not to think about him some, despite how much I would love to just blot him out entirely. My family still lives beside his parents, and seeing as how I live only three miles away, I visit quite often.

Thus, I see his mom and dad...a lot.

Which means I'm reminded of Rafe and everything we had and everything he destroyed on a whim.

Sure, the rage has subsided over the years. I've gotten control of that. So when I do happen to think of him, it's often in passing. I might be over at his parents' house to say hello, and see his graduation photo on their mantel, thinking to myself: *I wonder what Rafe's up to.* And then I put him out of my mind. Sometimes, I might think: *I wonder if he's caught a raging case of syphilis—which he'd deserve,* and then I'll hope that it's super annoying and itchy.

Okay, that's not entirely true. I've never been a vindictive person, and I don't wish him ill at all. But, damn...I'm just so angry at him right this moment, and sitting next to him in my car isn't helping matters at all. All of the ugly feelings are welling up inside of me and I'll be glad when I can get away from him.

To say that Rafe broke my heart would be the understatement of all time. He didn't just hurt me...he *destroyed* me. Crushed me so badly, he didn't even leave fragmented pieces of betrayal behind. No...he ground me to dust and then just walked away.

It took me a long time to get over him, to acknowledge that he didn't want me. Took me years to accept he didn't think I was good enough to join him on his journey through the professional hockey league. And it took some major soul-searching to find a measure of peace within the world around me, validation that I was a worthy woman.

The way we ended things was so contrary to everything we'd planned for our future. Those plans had unfurled over the years as we grew up together—first pledging to always be best friends, all the way through the blossom of glorious love where we promised to be there for each other until our dying days.

So many memories for me to recall any time I want to take a journey through my past with Rafe. Us playing in the woods, picking mushrooms, and poking bugs with sticks. Me forcing Rafe to play Barbies with me, only to agree to play GI Joe with him as a compromise. Summers were spent swimming at the YMCA and going to movies. In school, from as far back as I can remember, he was always my protector because, for some reason, I was an easy target for bullies. Then, in fifth grade, the inevitable first and experimental kiss. We both thought it was horribly gross.

We tried it again in seventh grade, and it wasn't so gross. By ninth grade, we were going steady and where one was, so was the other. Fingers laced, we'd strut the halls of our high school, and the message was clear to anyone that paid attention.

We were together, and always would be.

I went to every single one of Rafe's hockey games when he played locally, usually hopping in Brenda's minivan to ride with her. He was a hockey star, and I was popular by virtue of my association with him and growing into my odd looks in a way that people found striking. When he went off to juniors, I sometimes traveled with Brenda to see him as much as I could. We burned up the phone with calls, texts, and FaceTime. When he returned home after the season was over, we were inseparable, making up for lost time.

We were the quintessential golden couple. Prom king and queen. Most likely to live happily ever after. I was sitting by his side, his hand clutching mine so hard, I thought my fingers would break, when they called with his draft offer to the league. I shared in the same excitement as he did because we had planned for that moment. We'd spent so much time talking about what would happen if he ever made it to the professionals. I had doubts, but Rafe...never.

He'd straight-out asked me, "Poppy, you're coming with me, right? Wherever I land? Whatever city? You're coming with me, right?"

My answer was fast and easy. "Yes, Rafe. I'll follow you to the ends of the Earth."

Until he decided he didn't want me to follow him at all.

When he changed his mind—disregarding all our future plans—it came as such a shock I couldn't even understand it. Just two weeks before he was set to join his new team, he flat-out told me that he didn't want me to come.

I couldn't even process it. I was so hurt, so blinded by what I thought was a failure on my part to be the right woman for him, that I had trouble even fighting against it at first. I was just...numb.

Then, after a whole lot of crying in my mom's arms, I tried to rally a bit. Attempted to fight to keep him.

God, what ensued was awful. Without really even understanding why he was doing what he was to me, I tried to hold on to the illusion of happiness we had. It ended up being me...flat-out begging Rafe with all my might to change his mind. It was so ugly. The woman I am today is so ashamed of how pathetic I was back then, down on my knees, holding on to his legs, sobbing and begging him not to leave me behind.

My face heats up just from the memory of that pitiful eighteen-year-old girl who didn't understand her own worth. Who couldn't figure out that Rafe wasn't good enough for her, and not the other way around.

But I know it now.

Rafe shifts in his seat, gaze still on the scenery whizzing by. I steal a glance at him, irritated that he's only gotten better-looking over time. He's filled out...become brawnier, but it's the face that always gets me. Warm brown hair that always looks tousled and expressive hazel eyes.

Gone is the boyish hotness, and in its place is an incredibly handsome, rugged-looking man.

Hell, even his gorgeous looks piss me off, and I turn back to the road.

The silence between us should be welcoming, but in a way, it's grating. I'm torn between wanting to be a bitch to him because he deserves it and wanting to hug the hell out of him because of what he's going through right now. To complicate matters, I love his father, too. I'm grieving just as he is, and I can't even accept comfort from him, which I know he'll attempt to give me at some point. I figure I'll reconcile those conflicting feelings eventually.

I pull into our neighborhood. It's mostly modest split-levels built in the sixties on small lots shaded by oaks and pines. Rafe's house is the same dove gray it's always been, with burgundy shutters and a small slab concrete porch with three steps. My parents' house used to be a baby blue, but they just recently painted it white with black shutters. They added an iron railing to the porch, something my mom had wanted for years and my dad surprised her with.

I choose to park at my parents' home since I'll be joining them for dinner tonight—not that it matters. The parallel driveways actually run right beside each other, separated only by about three feet of new spring grass.

"Thanks for the ride," Rafe says without looking my way, and then he's out the passenger door. It's closed before I even get the engine shut off. By the time I'm stepping out, he's got his suitcase out of my rear hatch and is headed to his front porch.

I follow along behind, telling myself that it would be nice to check in on Jim and Brenda. Doesn't matter that I just looked in on them a few hours ago, which led to me being asked to pick up Rafe from the airport. Doesn't matter that Rafe and I aren't even on speaking terms really. I stick close to him as he bounds up the porch steps and drops his suitcase off to the side beside an empty planter.

He hesitates for just a moment, his hand inches from the storm door handle. His face angles my way, and I get a glimpse of hesitancy in his expression. It doesn't last but a second before his jawline hardens, and he pulls open the door. Without delay, he steps into the house, and for a moment, I lose sight of him.

I scramble...the screen door closing all the way. I wrench it open, finding that Rafe left the interior door open. There's nothing wrong with me barging into the Simmonses' home...I've been doing it for well over two decades, and no one expects me to knock.

I step into a small foyer from which a half staircase leads up to the living area, and a half staircase leads down to the basement level. I choose up, knowing that's where Rafe will find Jim in his cozy recliner, watching sports. It's where the recliner will eventually be replaced by a hospital bed once he loses mobility. I was there when Brenda sat down and talked with a hospice representative not long ago.

I trot up the steps—five in all—and round the banister that opens into a small living room.

I see Brenda first, pulling away from a hug with Rafe. He holds on to her just a bit longer than he might ordinarily, then releases her with a wan smile. She touches her fingertips to his cheek and steps away.

A lump forms in my throat as Rafe turns toward his dad. Jim struggles out of his recliner, his body becoming noticeably weaker every day. Brenda takes a step his way, intent on helping him up as she often does, I'm sure, but Rafe places a restraining hand on her shoulder. A silent plea to let his dad do it himself because he wouldn't want to look weak to his son.

Rafe's never been very close to his dad. Hasn't had to care for him the last few weeks as he started rapidly declining without even understanding why at first. But right now...in this moment...Rafe understands him better than any of us. As a man might understand another's need to be as strong as possible, despite the circumstances.

Jim scoots to the edge of the recliner, plants his slippered feet on the carpet, and pushes himself out of the chair. His clothes hang loosely on him, his lack of appetite for months raising all kinds of red flags for Brenda. Try as she might, she just couldn't get him to go see a doctor.

"Son," Jim says, his voice sounding strong. It's all for show because that's not usually how he sounds these days. Rafe will figure that out soon enough.

"Hey, Dad," Rafe replies softly, and in two big strides, he's bridged the gap between them. Both men open their arms, and then Rafe gently enfolds his dad in an embrace. They hug tightly and long, Rafe's face bending down to press into his dad's shoulder.

My eyes get misty as I realize I've never seen them hug before.

In my entire lifetime of knowing Rafe and his family, discovering that this is the first time I've ever seen the men embrace is a stark realization.

How did I not notice that before?

Was it because my eyes were so starry and dazzled by Rafe's brilliance that I didn't notice something as simple as a lack of physical connection between father and son?

I feel a bit more of my anger toward Rafe drain away, only to be immediately replaced by sympathy for what he must be feeling now.

That big clock now ticking down to an awful, painful conclusion that no one is ever ready for.

I imagine there might be a lot of regret on both sides, and I really hope they can make the most of their remaining time together.

Rafe is the first one to pull back, but he still holds on to his dad's shoulders, studying Jim's face. His lips quirk up, and he teases, "Your hair's getting grayer."

Jim tips his head back and gives a hoarse, frail laugh of delight.

I take that as my cue to leave. I'm not needed here right now. And besides, in addition to all of the heavy emotions swirling around in the house, I'm dealing with my own conflicts about Rafe's return.

Chapter 3

Rafe

The Cold Fury management offices are more traditional than the Vengeance's. Where the Vengeance executive suite is all airy with light colors and chrome, the Cold Fury décor is dark-paneled walls, thick, plush carpeting, and ambient lighting from wall sconces.

None of that matters to me, though. I'm just happy and grateful to be on this team. It's a miracle of sorts that I even made it here. The move was made after the trade deadline, which meant I wasn't eligible to play in the playoffs. As such, Dominik Carlson and Gray Brannon came up with a risky plan and maneuver to release me down to our minor league team on waivers. The same was done with my counterpart here at Cold Fury, Kane Bellan. Then, when the waiver time expired, both coaches snapped us up to join opposite teams. I'm sure other teams wanted us, but I expect that some palms were greased or something to make the switch happen as it did.

Regardless, I'm just so fucking relieved to be here. It means I get to spend time with my dad and continue playing hockey. I know it will end up being my saving grace throughout my dad's last days.

The receptionist in the lobby area of the executive suite looks up with a smile as I approach her desk. "Can I help you?"

"I'm Rafe Simmons," I tell her. "I'm supposed to meet with Gray Brannon this morning."

"Of course, Mr. Simmons," she says exuberantly, rising from her desk. "Ms. Brannon is expecting you and told me to bring you right back when you arrived. If you'll follow me, please."

She leads me down a hall to Gray's office, a luxurious space as traditionally styled as the rest of the suite. The receptionist gives a short rap on the door but doesn't wait for a response, merely pushes it open and steps inside to announce me.

I'm stunned to see Gray on the floor in front of her desk, playing with a baby, who is chewing on a wooden block.

Gray Brannon is a beautiful woman with fiery red hair and crystal green eyes. She's gorgeous, but it's not what she's typically known for. Instead, she's the first and only female general manager in the league, a former Olympic hockey player and bronze medalist who managed to lead the Cold Fury to back-to-back Cup championships since joining the team four years ago.

I guess I shouldn't be surprised to see her on the floor, performing just another duty of her incredibly busy and challenging life: mom. I know she and her husband—former Cold Fury goalie Ryker Evans— had the baby about eleven months ago.

Gray looks up and grins at me, a toothy welcome that's also wholly unapologetic. She's not sorry that she's on the floor with her kid rather than greeting me with a handshake. "Hey, Rafe. Come on in."

I step past the receptionist, who backs out but leaves the door open.

"Sorry about this." Gray waves at herself and her baby—a little boy who smiles up at me, all gums and drool. "Ryker is swinging by to pick Milo up, but he's running a few minutes late."

"No worries," I reply with an easy smile, clasping my hands in front of me, unsure of what I should do. I think this meeting is just a formality, although Gray and I have talked on the phone twice since I approached Dominik Carlson with my request to come to the Cold Fury.

There's a knock on the open door behind me, and I turn to see Alex Crossman walk in.

Alex is the captain of the team, one of the finest players in the league, and heads up the first line as the center. It's the same position I play, except on the second line.

"I was just walking by," Alex explains as he sticks his hand out to me. "Saw you in here and thought I'd officially welcome you to the team."

I shake his hand, and he gives mine a hearty pump. "Good to see you," I tell him.

I've met Alex on a few occasions at public events, and he's always been gracious. I'm excited to play under his leadership.

"Alex," Gray says, pulling Milo onto her lap. "Ryker's coming by to pick up the rug rat, but he's running late. Do you mind taking Rafe down to the locker room and showing him around? I'll be down later."

"Not at all," Alex replies easily and turns for the door. "Just headed there myself."

This isn't unexpected. We have a team skate in about half an hour, which will be just a light workout since there's a game tonight. The Cold Fury is taking on the Toronto Blazers tonight in the second game of the first round of the playoffs. The Cold Fury already took game one the day before last. While I won't be playing in tonight's game, I *will* be skating with the team to get my feet wet. Gray told me they expect me to head up the second line for game three in two days' time.

Today is more about meeting my teammates and establishing some chemistry with the rest of the guys on the second line.

"It was great meeting you, Gray," I tell her with an incline of my head that speaks to my gratitude. "I can't thank you enough for doing this."

Her face softens, and she pulls Milo in a little closer to her chest. "We're glad to have you. I hate the circumstances that brought you to the team, but we're all here to support you. That being said, we think you're a great addition, and will be of great benefit to us."

That's overly kind of her to say. It's going to be a bit of a transition for them to get used to me and my style of play. While Kane Bellan and I were a pretty even trade, there are slight differences. It's going to be a hindrance to the second line until we can gel—something that could happen within the first game, or several after.

Alex and I leave the executive suite. In the elevator heading down to the basement level that houses the locker room, he makes the overture that I'm sure I will get a lot today. "I'm really sorry to hear about your dad."

"Thanks," I reply with a smile I don't feel. "I appreciate it."

He studies me for a moment, a bit of calculation in his eyes. "Listen...I don't need to tell you that every player needs to play at an optimum level since we're in the playoffs. I also don't need to tell you that you've got some tough times ahead of you with your dad. If, at any time, your head isn't in the game the way it should be, I just need you to let us know. We've all got your back. You may be new to the team, but you are a brother to us now. If you need to take a step back, not one man on this team will ever begrudge you for taking the time you need for yourself and your family."

That was way more than I expected, and it touches me. He doesn't need to make those assurances. In fact, he has every right to be tough with me...acknowledging my shitty circumstances but making expectations clear—that I should be performing at peak level, no matter what.

"Thanks man… I really appreciate it," I say and he responds by clapping me on the shoulder.

The locker room is noisy and bustling. All of the players are in front of their wooden cubbies in various states of undress. The mood is jubilant, with a lot of laughing and joking going on. It reminds me of the Vengeance locker room, and I have a moment of intense longing for my old team.

Alex leads me over to my space, stopping along the way to do quick introductions. I already know many of my teammates, either from having played with them or against them, even dating back to my junior hockey days.

My cubby is open-faced, made of solid stained wood with an etched plaque that reads *R. Simmons* at the top. The equipment manager has been diligent. There's a practice uniform, the requisite pads, skates, and even my preferred brand of sticks waiting to be taped—which is something players usually do themselves.

A guy that I immediately recognize but have never had the opportunity to meet before is at his cubby to my right. Tall, with dark hair and the weirdest-looking golden eyes I've ever seen, ones that probably make women swoon, he shoots me an easy smile and sticks out his hand for me to shake. But it's Alex who makes the introduction. "Rafe… this is Zack Grantham. He'll be your left-winger."

We pump hands, and I tell him, "Hope I can fill Bellan's place and do it justice."

"I'm sure you can," he replies with an affirming nod of his head. "Looking forward to getting out on the ice with you."

Zack plops down on the bench that runs in front of our cubbies and starts to untie his shoelaces.

Another man approaches, and I recognize him as well. An icon, Garrett Samuelson is a first-line right-winger for the Cold Fury. He's joined by one of the best goalies in the league, the lynchpin of this team, Max Fournier.

We shake hands, and they are equally as warm and welcoming. The crowd starts to grow.

Max motions a guy over, and I can tell immediately that they're related. He introduces his brother, Lucas Fournier, to me.

"Glad to meet you." We shake hands, and I lean in with a conspiratorial grin. "Loved that hip check you put on Lars Nilsson a few weeks ago."

Lucas laughs and nods. "I bet you did."

Lars is a douchey player for the L.A. Demons. Last year, he pulled one of the lowest forms of violence I've ever seen in our league, and he did it with words.

Our first-line center for the Vengeance, Tacker Hall, was having a rough time. He lost his fiancée in a plane crash the year before, and as if that weren't bad enough, Tacker was the one piloting the aircraft, so he was dealing with loads of misplaced guilt.

At any rate, Tacker and Nilsson got into a scuffle on the ice, and rather than handle it the normal way by dropping gloves and duking it out, Nilsson made reference to Tacker killing his fiancée.

Tacker went ballistic and took Nilsson down to the ice, kneeing him in his head so severely he knocked him out cold. Tacker was suspended for several games, but in everyone's opinion, the ass-whipping was justified. I would have loved to have gotten a piece of him. I'm sure every player on our team would have.

"How is Tacker doing?" Lucas asks. Everyone in the league knows he's had demons to deal with.

"His stats say it all," I point out, and all the men standing around nod. Tacker is back at the top of his game, leading the league in points and dominating everyone on the ice.

Of course, I don't tell my new teammates how that most likely has everything to do with the way Tacker's heart healed in the time since he found love with Nora. They'd all think I was a pussy for saying something like that, but it's true. He's a new man since she came into his life, and I'll credit Dominik Carlson with that, as well. He pushed Tacker her way for some much-needed therapy, and what do you know...they fell in love.

The romantic in me can recognize that, even though seeing Calliope yesterday reminded me that I probably don't know shit about true love. Not the way Tacker and Nora do. It was brutal being back in Calliope's presence on top of having to deal with my dad. A double whammy of sorts, reminders of the losses I've suffered and the ones that are yet to come.

It's easy to put that all aside, though, as more people come up to introduce themselves, and I start to feel a tinge of excitement regarding the possibilities with this team. Veteran players that have helped to lead the Cold Fury to two Cup championships in the last two years. Men like Hawke Therrian, Roman Sykora, Van Turner, Reed Olson, and Marek Fabritis. I forgot just how stock-heavy this team was with star players. While only a few days ago, I thought it would be the Vengeance that would sweep everyone on the way to the championship, I now fully realize that I didn't take a step down when I switched teams. It was truly a lateral move, and the Cold Fury has just as much power as the Vengeance.

Despite the upheaval in my life and the pain I'll be facing, there is a bright spot on my horizon. I'm still very much in the mix for something good while playing for this team.

Chapter 4

Calliope

My phone rings and I consider ignoring it. I have my arms almost elbow-deep in dishwater, cleaning a stubborn pan. If it were any other ringtone, I likely would.

But it's Brenda calling. It could be something as simple as a chat, but chances are, it's something more important. With Jim having advanced cancer and an expected decline over the coming days, I can't afford to ignore Brenda's call.

Nor do I want to. The woman was my second mother growing up. I spent as much time in her house as mine, and there was a time I thought we'd be related by marriage, too. That clearly didn't happen, but when Rafe broke up with me, it didn't chill my relationship with his parents at all. If anything, it made it stronger. For the longest time after Rafe left to play professional hockey, I leaned on them because I missed him so badly. Throughout the years, our bond has continued to grow and develop, even as I moved on with my life. Despite the passage of time, Brenda is still like my second mom. She's also one of my mom's closest friends, and I love her dearly.

So of course I'll answer the phone. I quickly dry my arms and hands and nab the cell by the fourth ring, just before my voicemail picks up. "Brenda...hey...what's up?"

"It's Jim," she says, and there's no disguising the worry in her voice.

"He's having a hard time breathing, and I don't know what to do."

"What do you mean by *hard time breathing*?" I ask her, placing a palm on my kitchen counter.

"It's labored. There's a wheezing sound. And he's sort of lethargic."

"He probably needs to go to the hospital," I suggest.

While I don't mention the medical specifics, Jim is at the precipice of where his body will start betraying him. With the cancer having spread to his lungs, this is an expected symptom. But his other organs will also begin shutting down as they fight the unwinnable battle against the cancer. He'll need medical intervention to help make him more comfortable.

"He won't go, Calliope." She sighs, and I can just envision her pinching the bridge of her nose. It's what she does when she's frustrated. "And Rafe isn't here. If he were, maybe he could talk some sense into his dad."

"Tell you what," I say as I move through my apartment to the foyer, where I grab my purse and keys. "Let me come over and take a look at him. If he needs the hospital, we can call an ambulance. How does that sound?"

"Okay, yes," she breathes out in relief. "I'd appreciate it so much. I hate to bother you with—"

"It's never a bother, Brenda," I cut her off sharply. "Never. You call me, no matter what."

My heart almost breaks when all I hear through the line is a tiny hiccup of a sob.

"I'm on my way," I assure her.

I live nearby in an apartment complex just a few miles down the road. I chose the location because not only is it convenient for the hospital I work in, but it's also near my parents, who I'm incredibly close to. I eat dinner with them several times a week, and before Jim got sick, he and Brenda would sometimes join us.

I arrive at the Simmonses' house in less than five minutes. Brenda meets me at the front door and murmurs, "He's probably going to be angry I called you."

"I'm not worried about that," I assure her as I follow her up to the main level of the house. We turn left and move to the end of the hallway where their master bedroom is located.

The blinds are closed, and the interior is dim. Brenda moves around the bed to where Jim is lying on the far side and turns on the bedside lamp that has been draped with a fringy shawl to keep the light subdued.

She touches his shoulder and gives a gentle shake. "Jim... Calliope's here. She wants to check on you."

Jim's eyes flutter open, and he takes in a breath. I can hear the wheeze from across the room. He narrows his gaze on his wife a moment before his head turns my way. "I'm fine," he mutters and then looks back to Brenda. "You didn't need to bother her."

"Let me just take a look at you, Jim," I say as I move around the bed. Brenda steps out of my way, and I lean over, placing a hand on his forehead to see if he's running a fever.

In this moment, I'm only a family friend taking a look to render a non-medical opinion. I can't operate as a nurse, as his condition is outside my field of expertise. While I don't mind helping the family with decisions and talking things through, I can't give any type of expert opinion on his condition. Brenda probably doesn't really understand that, and I might need to clarify it at some point.

"He doesn't seem to be running a fever," I murmur and then drop my hand to his shoulder. "How hard is it to breathe, Jim?"

As if to prove nothing's wrong, he sucks in a big gulp of air and lets it out. "I'm fine. See."

I know he thinks he just performed a monumental feat for me, but even I can see that his lungs aren't filling to capacity. It's not a good sign. But now that I've seen him, I also don't think he needs immediate medical intervention. His color looks good, and he sounds pretty strong, actually.

Jim pushes himself up to lean against the headboard and wipes at his eyes as if to clear the sleep from them. "Listen...yes, I'm feeling a bit tired today. Doc said that would happen. But I'm just trying to rest up for the game tonight."

"Game?" I ask, turning my gaze to Brenda.

She gives a small shake of her head. "Technically, it's Rafe's first game with the Cold Fury. He's actually been at the arena this morning for his first team practice and getting to know the guys. He should be home any moment to hang out for a bit before he heads back for the game."

"And I want to watch the game on TV, so I'm just trying to get some rest," Jim gripes. "And I can't do that when the two of you are hovering over me. Now, I'm tired and want to nap a bit more."

"Fine," Brenda exclaims, holding up her hands in defeat. "Rest. I'll wake you up for lunch in a bit, okay?"

"Okay," he mutters and then gives her an apologetic smile. "And sorry I'm a grump."

"I've lived with your grumpy butt for almost thirty years," she replies affectionately. "I'm used to it."

Brenda and I leave the room, and she shuts the door behind us. "Want a cup of tea?"

"Sure," I reply, not really having anything else to do today except clean my kitchen. I'd actually planned to hang out at my place and read a book or watch some TV. I'm pretty low-maintenance on my days off and enjoy chilling more than anything.

I sit at the table while Brenda puts the kettle on. She's the one who got me into drinking tea years ago when I was still in high school. It always made me feel so adult and part of her family to sit at the table and sip as we talked. Of course, back then, we talked a lot about Rafe because he was the center of both our worlds.

"Is this it?" Brenda asks as she comes to join me at the table while the water heats.

The question may seem vague, but I get what she's asking. She wants to know if we're at the beginning of the end.

Before I can answer, the front door opens, and Rafe calls out in an exaggerated Cuban accent a la Ricky Ricardo, "L-u-u-u-c-y... I'm home."

I can't help but smile, and my gaze meets Brenda's. Rafe always used to do that when he came home from school in the afternoons.

"In the kitchen, honey," Brenda calls back to him.

We can hear Rafe bounding up the stairs, and as he comes into view, his eyes immediately lock on mine. Of course he knew I was here, my Pathfinder is in the driveway.

"What's going on?" he asks, letting the gear bag he's holding drop to the floor. His gaze flits from me to his mom.

She smiles at him, wan and fatigued. "Your dad's having a bad day. I asked Calliope to come by and check on him."

Rafe's eyes snap to me, locking on hard. "And?"

"He's having a hard time breathing—"

"Why?" he demands, his brows furrowing deeply. "I mean...I don't understand a goddamn thing about any of this."

"The cancer has spread to his lungs and his liver—"

"No," Rafe barks at me, looking wildly between his mother and me. "I don't understand how this happened. How did it get this bad, this fast?"

There's a world of recrimination in that statement, and he immediately flushes, a guilty expression on his face.

"Sorry," he mutters and spins on his heel, walking right out of the kitchen and trotting down the stairs.

Brenda starts to rise from the table to go after him, but I beat her to it, placing a hand on her shoulder. "Let me. I think he needs a rational explanation, and I can give that to him without too much emotion."

Because really...we're nothing to each other, so I'm perfect for the job.

Brenda nods, and I follow Rafe out of the house, expecting to find him in his mom's car. I assume his vehicle might be coming via freight carrier from Arizona at some point, or hell...maybe he's just going to buy a new one now that he's relocated. It's not like he can't afford it.

Instead, I find Rafe sitting on the top step of the porch, arms crossed over his knees and staring out at the street. He glances up at me and says, "I wasn't blaming anyone."

"I know that," I reply softly and take a seat beside him. "And I think that maybe you really *don't* have all the information you need to understand what's going on. So what can I do to clear things up?"

His expression morphs into relief. "Just explain the disease to me. How come he's so bad off? How come there's no hope?"

"Pancreatic cancer is very aggressive," I tell him bluntly. "There's no telling exactly how long your dad was having symptoms before they were even noticeable to your mom. But eventually, they got to the point where they couldn't be ignored. I know there was some back pain, which was at first discounted as aging. Then he lost his appetite, which caused him to lose weight. We thought that might be a bit of depression because he had to cut back on his work from the back pain. Your mom tried to get him to go to the doctor, but you know your dad...he didn't even go get a physical each year. He hated going to the doctor."

"What made him finally go?" he asks me. "These are all details that were kept from me, I'm assuming because my mom didn't want to worry me or because my dad and I just didn't have a close enough relationship for him to confide."

"His skin started turning yellow, so I think that ultimately scared him enough to go get checked out."

"And by then, it was too late?" he guesses.

"It had already spread to his liver and lungs," I explain to him. I went with Brenda and Jim—at their request—to meet with the oncologist. "He was offered chemo, but it wasn't going to buy him much time, and he didn't want to deal with the side effects."

Rafe lets out a gust of frustrated breath. I believe all family members struggle with the choice to undergo chemo or not. Knowing it couldn't fix Jim's problem but merely buy him precious moments, the trade-off was the side effects for him.

"Your dad really considered the options," I tell Rafe, who twists his neck to finally give me his attention. "He weighed the pros and the cons and, ultimately, he decided not to do the chemo."

"I was never involved in that conversation," he replies bitterly, thus revealing the source of his discontent: the fact that his opinion didn't matter.

I reach out and touch my hand to his arm. "It wouldn't have mattered. Your mom tried to talk him into the chemo. It's what she wanted, but not what *he* wanted."

Rafe stares at me for a long moment, clearly at war with his emotions. Finally, his expression smooths into one of acceptance, and he nods.

It's neither awkward nor unsettling that we simply stare at each other, neither of us needing to say anything. I wait to see if he has more questions, but the sound of tires rasping on cement nabs our attention, and we turn to see a black Corvette pulling into my parents' driveway.

My spine stiffens as the car comes to a stop, and the driver's door opens. "Shit," I mutter.

Rafe stands, and I do the same as I see my ex-boyfriend unfurl his big body from the little sports car. I always thought he looked ridiculous crammed into that sardine can.

"Who's that?" Rafe asks, his tone guarded, and his stance vigilant.

"My ex," I mutter and move down the steps, intent on getting him right back in his car and on his way. "I'll be right back."

He shuts the door as I walk toward him, his gaze flicking from me to Rafe, where he still stands on the porch.

"Who's that?" Grant demands, pointing an angry finger over my shoulder at Rafe.

"A friend," I tell him curtly, offering no more explanation because it's none of his business. We broke up over two weeks ago, but Grant just doesn't seem to get it.

"We need to talk," he says, shooting one last look in Rafe's direction before bringing his attention to me. "I thought maybe we could run out, grab a beer or something."

"No, Grant." I sigh with extreme frustration. "We can't do that because we are over. Now you need to leave."

I get a smarmy, disbelieving smile in return. "I think if you just listen to me—"

"She said you need to leave," Rafe says from very close behind me, and I cringe. Grant is a complete hot-head, and this could totally escalate. I turn slowly, intent on making Rafe leave, but he refuses to look at me. Instead, he glares daggers at Grant.

"Who the fuck are you?" Grant bellows, taking a threatening step toward Rafe.

I give a very brief glance at Rafe, whose face contorts with anger, before I spin on Grant and slam my hands to his chest. I give him a solid push back, and he only moves because I catch him off guard.

Furious, I snarl at him. "You need to leave now, or I'm calling the police. You are not wanted here, nor do you have any right to be here."

Thankfully, Rafe remains silent, and I'm grateful because just one word from him could whip up Grant's temper. But, apparently, my threat to call the police has some effect because Grant glares at me before spinning on his foot and muttering, "Don't know why I put up with you, crazy bitch..."

His words were loud enough for Rafe to hear. While we may have been broken up for the past eight years, I know the man well, and I know how he was raised. He'll never stand for a man calling a woman a bitch.

I spin quickly toward Rafe, and just as I did with Grant, I slam my hands to his chest and warn him, "Don't even think about it."

Rafe leans into me, his eyes hot on Grant, but he heeds my warning. I glance over my shoulder, and I'm relieved to see Grant getting into his car. He cranks it, revs the engine until it whines in a vulgar display of male ego, and then he peels out of the driveway, proving that he's a child and that it was a good thing I broke up with him.

"What a fucktard, Calliope," Rafe mutters with condescension, and I whip my gaze back to him. "Seriously...what did you see in him?"

I give Rafe a hard push he's not expecting. He takes two steps back and gives me an astonished look.

"You're as big an asshole as he is," I growl at him. "And it's none of your business what I may or may not have seen in him."

"Why are you angry at me?" he asks, completely oblivious. "I had your back, you know."

"Because it's not your place to have my back anymore," I retort, pointing an angry finger at him. "You lost that right eight years ago when you dumped me without an explanation."

Instantly, Rafe's eyes fill with regret, and the sympathetic look he gives me causes my anger to boil over. "I'm so sorry—"

"Don't," I exclaim, holding one palm out to him. "Don't you dare try and apologize to me now. You lost that right, too. And, besides...it's too late."

Rafe's mouth shuts, but he still regards me with regret written all over his face. I can't stand it.

I move past him and make my way back into Brenda and Jim's house. I'm going to have my cup of tea like I would on any other occasion while visiting. Then I'm going to ignore this man who still manages to provoke me and stretch all my emotions to the extreme.

Chapter 5

Rafe

I step out onto the ice, joining my team for pre-game warmup to the screams of fans and blaring rock music. I returned home to Raleigh a week ago, and much has happened since. I've assimilated well with the Cold Fury, and I'm getting ready to play in my third game for my new team. It's the fifth game of this playoff round, and I'm confident that we can seal the deal tonight.

Each round of the Cup playoffs is seven games, and the first team to win four takes the round. The Cold Fury earned home-ice advantage, so the first two games—which we won—were in Raleigh. The next two games were in Toronto, my first to play with the team, and we split those, losing a heartbreaker in overtime the night before last. Tonight, we're back on home ice, and we're up three games to one. We're determined and fired up for victory. Sometimes, you could just feel it in your bones.

I'm on a little bit of a high tonight. Got a call from one of my former teammates, Aaron Wylde, this afternoon. He called to check in on me. I've received dozens of calls, texts, and emails from many of my Vengeance teammates, but Wylde has reached out the most. He went through something similar off the ice, so more than anyone else, he understands the myriad emotions I'm feeling. I'm really grateful for his concern, and he's been a great source of valuable advice on how to process everything.

The one thing he can't help me with are the feelings I have regarding Calliope. Wylde's never had a serious relationship...never been in love. He has no interest in settling down, and thus can't comprehend how I've gone years carrying a torch for one woman. Not that any of my former teammates really know that. I never told any of them about Calliope and how I left her behind. I never divulged that she was my one true love, and the different women they saw me date over the years were nothing compared to her.

As I skate around the ice, letting my legs acclimate, my eyes scan the arena—the section between the upper and lower decks where I know my parents will be—and I try to discern if Calliope is with them. I left a ticket for her, leaving it up to my mom to pass on the invitation to tonight's game, but I have no clue if she accepted. We haven't exactly been on speaking terms since I stepped on her toes when her douche of an ex-boyfriend showed up. That was six days ago, and for almost four of those days, I was in Toronto playing the two road games. I have no clue what she's feeling, or if we're even back on speaking terms.

My mom has freely shared information about her—though not because I asked. Only because hospice came out to my parents' house while I was in Toronto and got things set up for Dad, and apparently, Calliope was there to help them navigate the overwhelming amount of information they received.

Mom said they met with their hospice nurse for almost three hours to go over everything. They learned things that no family member should ever have to know, including the physical changes that will happen to Dad as he starts to die. Mom promised she'd go over everything with me when I returned to Raleigh, and the thought of it made me want to vomit.

I've been back one day, and she hasn't brought it up. Neither have I. I want to get through tonight's game, hopefully seal up this round with a win. Then I can put some energy into it since we'll have a few days off until the next round starts.

I look back up at the section where I think my dad will be. It's a seating area available to people in wheelchairs, and part of the hospice package included a shiny new wheelchair. I'm not sure whether or not he's going to use it, but when I left for the arena today, he was adamantly opposed to it.

Granted...he seemed to be having a really good day. Woke up with energy and actually ate a decent breakfast. According to my mom, who got the information from the hospice nurse, he will have good days and bad days, and it will be unpredictable. She said it can cause a lot of anxiety for us because the good days will inevitably lead to false hope. My mom told me today that we need to be grateful for every good moment he has, knowing that there are far more bad ones to come in the future. It was plain talk, but I appreciated it.

When I left for the arena, Mom was pushing for him to use the wheelchair, her argument being that he could be worn out by the time the game was over. My dad told her he was feeling pretty damn good and didn't want to have the assistance unless he had to.

My personal opinion was that Dad should make the decision, but I didn't voice it. But I did tell my mom that she should just let him go without it. I promised her that if he ran into trouble after the game and didn't have the strength to walk out, I would get help. That seemed to put her at ease enough and because I can't seem to locate them in the wheelchair area where they would be if he brought it, I assume they're in the ticketed seats. I don't know what those seats are just yet since I don't have access to annual passes because I'm so new to the team, and their tickets were handled through will-call.

It's enough to know that they're here to watch me. I'll take any games my dad can make it to and cherish it more than I ever did in the past.

Even more than that first professional game I played when I signed with Calgary. My parents both flew there to watch me play. I'd splurged and bought them first-class airline tickets and put them up in a luxury hotel, proud of the money I was making. I had a limo bring them to the game, and I was on cloud nine stepping out onto that ice, knowing they were there to watch me.

Knowing my dad was there, taking the time from his busy work schedule to come and see his son play.

That moment seems almost dull in comparison to right now, knowing that this could potentially be the last game my dad watches me play live.

I'm going to make it count. I'm pumped and ready to go. In fact, this feeling...the adrenaline and surge of pure joy for the game is the only thing that makes the deep despair in the pit of my stomach that never quite goes away even bearable. It's hard to let a few minutes go by without thinking about the fact that my dad will soon be gone, and my relationship with him is on borrowed time.

Hockey is the only thing keeping me sane right now.

* * * *

I can still feel my teammates patting me on the helmet after I scored the game-winner tonight, and the taps of their sticks against my calves. The win is a rush that doesn't die down easily, and I finally feel completely in sync with my new team.

Zack invited me out for some beers tonight, but I declined, not hiding the truth.

"Going home to spend time with my dad," I told him. "He had a good day today, and I want to take advantage of it."

Of course he understood, and I knew this by the way he clasped my shoulder with a solemn nod.

Now, though, when I pull into my parents' driveway, the adrenaline high from winning the game and thus the playoff round for my team, starts to fizzle.

There is nothing inside to be excited about. There is no joy. No solace, security, or hopefulness.

Nothing but a dying man.

With a sigh, I get out of my car. It was delivered a few days ago, along with all of my furniture and belongings. I placed all of it in storage, having no intention of getting my own place just yet.

For the immediate future, I want to spend my time at my parents' home—my childhood home—so I can be as close to my dad as possible. After the hockey season wraps up, there's no telling if I'll stay with the Cold Fury or get traded elsewhere. My deal was only for the remainder of the season, and while I'm playing well so far, that doesn't really mean anything.

Trudging up the sidewalk with my gear bag over my shoulder, I'm both reticent and eager to walk in. I hate looking at all of the medical equipment now taking up the entire living room except for the recliner, loveseat, and TV, but I'm looking forward to spending the rest of the evening with my dad. Time is way too precious.

I unlock the door with my key and push it open slowly. The hinges are well oiled and don't make a sound. It's important to be quiet, as my dad's bedroom is now the living room, and he may be sleeping.

Dropping my bag in the foyer, I creep up the carpeted half-flight of stairs and peek around the banister. My dad's actually in his recliner watching the news. I move fully into his line of vision, and he startles slightly, not having heard me come in.

His face morphs and a wide smile breaks out. "There's the hottest new star for the Cold Fury."

"You were able to come, then?" I ask.

My dad nods with a lopsided grin. "Even walked myself. Didn't need that damn wheelchair."

"Awesome." My return smile doesn't feel as forced as it's been. I think I'm learning to relish his good days. I point toward the kitchen. "Hey...I'm going to grab a beer. Want anything?"

"I'll take one, too," my dad replies, lowering the leg support of the recliner so he can sit more upright.

For a moment, I wonder if he's even allowed to have a beer. He's on some medications, but regrettably, I don't know what they're for. Part of me feels I should question him, but another part of me doesn't want to offend him either.

In the end, I figure my dad knows what's best for him. His mental faculties are still all in check, and if a dying man wants a beer, he gets a beer.

I nab two ice-cold bottles from the fridge, my mom having thoughtfully stocked a six-pack of my favorite brew. Skirting around the hospital bed in the middle of the room, I hand my dad a bottle before collapsing back onto the loveseat, directly opposite his recliner.

He holds up his bottle. "Cheers, and congrats on an awesome game."

I lift my beer up in acknowledgment. "Thanks. I'm really glad you were able to come."

Dad's expression turns thoughtful, his mouth turning slightly downward. "I missed way too many games while you were growing up."

I don't know how to respond because there's no mistaking the apologetic tone in his words. Does he want some type of absolution?

"Nah," I drawl with a wave of my hand.

"Missed so many," he replies sadly, his eyes locking with mine. "You see, son, when you're faced with death, you reflect on your life, and all of the regrets start pushing their way to the surface. I just need you to know...it's a big regret of mine. One of my biggest, I guess you'd say. That I didn't spend enough time with you as a dad should with his son. I always put work first, and well...if I could change that, I would.

But I can't, so the next best thing is to tell you I'm sorry for it."

"Dad," I say, but my voice cracks. I don't want to have this conversation, not because it's difficult for me to handle, but because I don't want his last days—precious hours and minutes—to be made up of him feeling bad about his choices.

He holds up a hand, indicating that he wants me to listen. "The hospice nurse spent a lot of time with us, kind of educating us on how it's going to happen. There's no telling how fast it's going to come...the end. I don't want to leave anything unsaid. So, over the next few days...weeks...whatever I have left, I might want to talk about some of these things. It's important to me."

I swallow hard past the lump of emotion clogging my throat and manage to croak, "Yeah...of course, Dad."

And thus, I learn a lesson. You hear it all the time. Many people say it, but really...it's never impacted me much.

Don't take a single moment for granted.

The regret my dad is wallowing in, and without any time to rectify it, is heartbreaking to watch. The least I can do for him is listen when he wants to unburden himself.

Chapter 6

Calliope

I'm exhausted, having pulled a double shift to cover a co-worker struck with the stomach bug. I'm a big believer in stepping up to help out with things like that because well...karma is out there floating around, and I don't want to offend her.

The hot shower I just took didn't refresh me but instead made me feel drowsy. My bed is calling, and I should listen.

Instead, I pull on a pair of worn jeans, a T-shirt, and a pair of sandals. I give my hair a quick, rough dry and, because there's a chance that Rafe will be there, I put on some mascara and lip gloss.

Yes, I'm going over to his parents' house because I want to check in on Brenda and Jim. I want to see how hospice got everything set up and make sure they're adjusting. The fact that I'm putting on lip gloss and mascara because Rafe will probably be there is like a pebble stuck in my shoe. It's annoying as hell that I even care what he thinks about my looks because I'm absolutely not interested in him in that way.

Not really.

I mean...I appreciated his intervention with Grant the other day, even though I was equally annoyed that he thought it was his place to step in. And I have to admit to being swayed by sympathy a tremendous amount. Knowing what he's getting ready to go through with his dad makes my anger toward him seem silly. We broke up a long time ago, and while I hated everything about that experience, it did help me become the woman I am today.

I'm independent, strong, and when a man doesn't treat me right—hello, Grant—I cut that shit out of my life because I know I'm better than that. I deserve more than the way Rafe dumped me or the way Grant treated me—as if I was a lesser, second-rate person merely because of my gender.

Mostly, though, I'm softening to Rafe—potentially being a friend to me again—because we are getting ready to share a loss together. I love his dad, not as much as he does and in a different way, but the Simmonses are part of my family unit. I've been involved heavily in Jim's most recent medical issues, they've turned to me for explanation and comfort, and I intend to be there for them going forward. In my heart, I want to offer the same to Rafe because I can't bear to think of the pain he'll be facing and thus...I have to put aside the bitter feelings I've clearly been harboring all these years.

So I leave my apartment and make the short drive to the Simmonses' house. Because I want to be there for all of them through this, and it has nothing to do with karma. It has to do with love.

I pull into my parents' short driveway, unconcerned with blocking them in or out. They went on a short trip to Wilmington for the weekend. Both of them have semi-retired, and they love taking weekend trips to the coast. I'm thinking they'll want to fully retire there before long.

I make a mental note to grab today's mail for them before I leave and head into the Simmonses' house. As usual, I give just a short knock to announce my presence, but I walk right in.

"It's me," I call out, not overly loud but enough to drift up the stairs.

"Come on up," Brenda responds. I can tell from the direction of her voice and the slight echo that she's in the kitchen. They have a big skylight over the sink area and over the years, I've come to recognize the way voices carry from that part of the house.

I come around the banister, my gaze going to the hospital bed in the middle of the living room. Jim is in it, and I'm struck by how small he seems all of a sudden. I know he went to the hockey game last night to watch Rafe play, and Brenda was so happy with how well he did. He insisted on walking, declining the use of the wheelchair that had been supplied by hospice.

But now I can see him sleeping deeply, undisturbed by my entrance into his home. He makes a slight snoring sound, and his chest rises and falls deeply.

I look away and move into the kitchen. Brenda's at the sink, rinsing out a cup. Her gaze lands on me, and I see the worry there.

He was good yesterday, and now today...

"This is typical," I remind her, answering the question in her eyes. She knows he's going to have good and bad days. The hospice nurse was very clear about that and soon, the bad will outnumber the good. "Take the good days and treasure them."

Her eyes mist up, and she nods.

"Where's Rafe?" I ask her. Since they clinched this round of the playoffs, he has the next four days off, and I just assumed he'd be by his dad's side.

Brenda's gaze shifts to peer out the window over the sink that overlooks the back yard. "He's out there, weeding."

I move over to the sliding glass doors on the other side of the small kitchen table and look out past the deck. Sure enough, Rafe is on his hands and knees in one of Brenda's flowerbeds, now only sporting daffodils that lost their blooms a few weeks ago. I imagine Brenda hasn't been in much of a gardening mood since they got Jim's diagnosis.

I study Rafe.

We've been apart for eight years, and yet I clearly recognize the frustration and anger in his posture. The way his upper back is hunched, shoulders dipped and frozen in place. His plucking at the weeds is stiff and mechanical.

"He's been out there since his dad fell asleep a few hours ago," she says, her voice tinged with sadness. "He sat by that hospital bed for a full hour, waiting for him to wake back up. I can tell he's having a hard time processing all this."

My heart cramps a bit. "He's had such huge upheaval in his life," I murmur to Brenda. "Finding out about Jim, moving to a new team. I'm surprised he's not pulling your good plants out."

Brenda chuckles. "Me, too."

I turn to her, struck by the worry on her face for her son. She has enough on her plate without having to shoulder concern for Rafe, too.

"I have an idea," I say, unsure how wise this will be, but committed all the same.

Without another word, I open the sliding glass door and step out onto the sunny deck. It's elevated and several steps down. The slapping of my sandals against the weathered wood catches Rafe's attention, and his neck twists to take me in.

I would have felt better if I'd seen some emotion on his face—

irritation at me, or pain over his father. I would even feel good at seeing something like regret or longing for better days. Instead, I see nothing.

His eyes are flat, and his mouth slackens before he turns back to his weeding. I watch him as I approach, and see he's doing nothing more than rearranging small nuggets of bark mulch. I have to wonder if he's completely shut down.

"Get up," I command as I reach where he's hunched over in the flowerbed.

His body jerks as his head snaps my way. "What?"

"Get up," I repeat. "Let's go."

"Go where?"

"Out of here," I reply and then turn on my heel. I make my way back up the staircase of the deck and head into the kitchen.

"What's going on?" Brenda asks softly as I slide the door closed behind me.

I smile at her, my expression reassuring and slightly mischievous. "I'm taking your son out for some fresh air. Tell him I'll be waiting in my car."

* * * *

"I can't believe this is still here...untouched."

I glance at Rafe as he gazes out over Old Man Podden's pond. It sits on the back of a large tobacco and corn farm at the edge of Wake and Franklin counties. He's surprised because the capital city of Raleigh has been expanding outward, and all the country farms have been sold off to real estate developers.

But Podden's pond remains, and it's a well-protected secret. Podden sold off most of his farm but kept a small portion of land, about twenty acres with the original homestead. I have unfettered access to it because my dad has been Podden's mechanic for decades. The pond itself is a hidden treasure, secluded by a copse of pine and oak trees, an old, abandoned dirt road the only way to access it.

"Raleigh is growing so fast," I agree before tipping my beer back to drain the rest.

I backed my Pathfinder up to a cleared spot near the edge of the pond. It's close enough that if we had fishing poles, we could cast right from the rear where we're now sitting.

Rafe mimics my action, emptying his bottle. We've always drunk beer at the same rate...not too fast and not too slow. Granted, it wasn't like we drank a lot, but we had our ways of getting our hands on it, even back then.

He reaches behind him to the cooler we grabbed from my parents' garage, which we filled with ice and beer from a convenience store as we traveled up Route 1 to the pond. He pulls out two more bottles—our second beer each—twists off the caps, and hands me one.

It's weird how, without thought, we both automatically tap the glass necks together and say, "Cheers."

It's what we always used to do when we slipped away to the pond with a picnic basket and ice-cold Cokes.

Rafe spares me an awkward smile. I can see in his expression that he knows perhaps the fond memory might provoke more bitter feelings within me, a potent reminder of what's been lost.

Quite the opposite happens, though.

I feel the need to reminisce. "Remember my senior skip day?"

Rafe chuckles, and his smile becomes relaxed. "How everyone headed east on I-40 to the beach, but we came here instead?"

I give him a look of faux reprimand. "You were home visiting from Green Bay and said it would be romantic, but really...you just wanted to get me alone so you could get in my pants."

Rafe snorts. "It *was* romantic, and let's be honest...you wanted in my pants just as much."

I giggle because it's true. Once we relieved each other of our virginities at age seventeen—even though he's almost ten days younger than I am—we couldn't get enough of each other. The only problem was, being next-door neighbors with our parents' noses always in both our businesses, our opportunities to be together were not plentiful.

So senior skip day was a golden opportunity. While my entire senior class headed to the beach for a day of frolicking and fun, Rafe and I wanted nothing more than to be together.

Intimately? Yes.

But more than that. We were settled—really at our happiest—when it was just us.

"It's a good thing we didn't go to the beach that day," I muse, taking another long pull off my beer.

"No kidding." He laughs, and I join in.

That turned out to be a very bad idea for a lot of students. Turned out the underground plan for every senior to skip class on a coordinated day in favor of spending the day at the beach with a whole lot of underage drinking didn't turn out so well for those who went. Our vice principal, Mr. Henkel, had somehow intercepted the plan. He was waiting at the high-rise bridge that crossed to Topsail Island with a list of every person's make and model of car.

He made a note of every single one and then managed to track down every party on the north side of the island at one of the public beach accesses. There, he handed out detention slips and called everyone's parents.

Sure, I skipped that day too, with Rafe at my side, but we weren't busted at the beach with beers in hand, dealing with subsequent calls to our parents.

Instead, we enjoyed a quiet day to ourselves, fishing on Podden's pond, eating ham sandwiches and drinking ice-cold Cokes, and we made love in the back of his car without a care in the world. It was one of the best days of my life, honestly.

And not something I really should be thinking of.

Rafe and I sip at our beers, and finally, I poke at him a bit. "So, what's the deal with tearing up your mom's flowerbed in the back yard today?"

It's a roundabout way of me asking him how he's doing, and he knows exactly what I'm angling for as his eyes meet mine, his expression not one of forthcoming information but questions of his own.

I can see them, brutally clear, even if he doesn't voice them aloud.

Do you really want to know?

Why should I tell you? We're less than friends these days.

Can I really share this with you, or will you turn your anger back on me? Because I really can't handle much more grief these days.

I reach out to him, placing my hand on his thigh and giving it a pat. There's nothing sexual about the gesture, but I hope the solid warmth of my touch, and the fact that I don't hesitate to reach out to him means that he can trust me with his sorrows.

"Lay it on me, Rafe," I murmur quietly. "I know you can't burden your mom. I know it's hard to talk to your dad. I'm here, and I'm listening."

Rafe physically deflates, his posture sagging as he cradles his beer bottle between his legs and stares at it. He doesn't look my way, but his words are only for me. "I feel hopeless. Out of control."

The power of his admission humbles me. I know Rafe as well as anyone, and he's a strong, proud man. He never admits to weakness, always stoically carrying whatever burden is on his shoulders. Even back when we were together, he didn't show his vulnerability to me because he didn't want to weigh me down.

That he's actually sharing with me now causes a shift within me that feels like loose sand on a beach dune.

He's actually sliced himself open to let me see a part of him that, no matter how close we were before, I'd never been given the privilege of observing.

The fact that he's doing so now causes more of the walls I erected to crumble, revealing more of my current self to him as well. It's like peeling away a protective hide, leaving me raw and exposed.

I swallow past the lump of emotion in my throat and try to give him the best advice I can. "I expect that's normal given your situation. And I expect there's no easy fix. I don't think you really need me telling you this, but I'll say it anyway. You need to make the most of what time you have left."

His gaze comes to me slowly.

Painfully.

The naked grief in his eyes touches me so deeply, I lean into him. "You've got this, Rafe. I'll help you through it."

"Why would you?" His disbelief is evident. It's warranted, as well.

"Because, no matter what, I guess I still care about you. And I care deeply for your parents. You know that's never changed. Let me be here for you. You only have to tell me what you need, and I'll give it."

I'm not prepared for the flash of heat in his eyes, nor am I ready for the way my blood quickens from it.

"I need to feel something more than grief and sadness," he says bluntly. And then with challenge in his tone, he adds, "That may be the beer talking."

My mouth curves into an unbidden smile. Rafe's wit has always been effortless, his charm foolproof. It makes me want to play along, and that's probably the beer talking on my part.

Surely a kiss couldn't hurt, though. Take his mind off his problems for a bit. And it's practically a harmless gesture. It's not like we haven't kissed before, and we both know that it won't go anywhere past a mere touching of our lips.

But as I lean farther into him, I know that's likely the biggest lie I've ever told myself.

Chapter 7

Rafe

The past eight years of my life melt away when Calliope's lips touch mine.

Gone.

My entire professional hockey career fades.

The women I've dated over time...faceless.

The money I've made, unimportant.

Fuck, I'd forgotten how good she tastes. Her tongue touches mine, and when an electric surge of longing pulses through me, I realize we are in dangerous territory. Calliope has no clue that I've carried an agonizing torch of desire for my first true love all these years. She can't understand the depth of my feelings, and if I don't draw away now, this could be disastrous.

She'll never accept the truth.

I pull away, my eyes immediately taking her in.

I see eyes half-closed, a small smile playing on her mouth, and a tiny exhale of something that I can't quite put my finger on.

Disappointment?

Regret?

Her eyelids flutter open, and her hazel-green eyes stare at me. Confusion sets in. "What's wrong?"

Only about a million things.

"I don't want to take advantage of you," I reply.

Her chin jerks, and by the expression on her face, I can tell that thought never crossed her mind. Still, I hold her gaze.

Calliope, never one to back down, returns the look just as steadily.

Finally, she says, "I know I shouldn't even be attracted to you after..."

Her words crumble, drift away. And yet, she doesn't drop her gaze from mine. She inhales a fortifying breath and then lets it out slowly. "I hated you for a very long time. And I'm ashamed of that because I was raised to never hate. But you hurt me so badly, and I went years without knowing what was so wrong with me that—"

"Nothing was wrong with you," I exclaim, my hand shooting out to clasp the back of her neck. She finally tries to avert her gaze, attempting to turn her head. I hold tightly, squeezing her neck gently and finally, she gives me her regard again. "I thought I was doing what was best for you."

Incredulity morphs her features, and her mouth opens in shock. "What was best for me? You crushed me."

"Christ," I mutter and frame her face with my hands. "I didn't think you would follow your dreams if you were following mine."

"That makes no sense," she blurts.

"It did to me back then," I reply bitterly. "You had big plans, Poppy. Nursing school. It was all you ever dreamed of. And yet you and I were so tied up in each other, I thought you'd lose sight of that. Moving away with me to Calgary so suddenly...you wouldn't have had time to enroll in school, and I just thought that if you got off track with your college plans, you wouldn't ever get back on. So I made the decision to leave you behind. I thought it was what was best for you, and that had to take precedence over what I wanted."

I'm stunned when Calliope's eyes flash with fury, and she knocks my hands away from her face. "You egocentric, sexist pig. How dare you decide what's best for me? How dare you think that I didn't have the fortitude to pursue my dreams while helping you follow yours at the same time?"

And, fuck...there it is. The source of my regret all these years. Because while I thought for quite a while that I was doing the right thing, deep down, I knew I never gave her the credit she deserved.

"I'm sorry," I offer. No truer words have ever been spoken. "I'm so very sorry. I got it wrong. So very fucking wrong."

"You're goddamned right you did," she seethes and scrambles from the back of the Pathfinder. She whirls to face me, hair flying, and eyes spitting sparks of wrathful fury. "You refused to even have a conversation with me about it. I begged you to tell me why you were making the decision, and all you said was that you changed your mind about wanting me to come with you. Do you know how devastating that was?"

"It was devastating to me, too, Poppy," I tell her.

She points a finger my way, wags it as if she's chastising a small child. "Oh, no, you don't. Don't you dare call me Poppy. You don't get to do that anymore."

I hold up my hands for a moment in silent surrender and hop to the ground beside her. She's magnificent in her rage, never having been more beautiful as she expels all of her anger at me.

But I want to calm this down. We're actually communicating, and I realize now that this is my chance to try and make things right with and for her. Make her realize that what I did, I did out of love.

I extend a hand to her. "Calliope..."

She takes a quick step back as if touching me would be a vile affront. Her second step back, and her sandaled foot comes right down on the edge of the pond bank. Dewy grass and mud take her hostage, and she starts to tumble backward.

I lurch for her, latching on to her wrist, but she tries to avoid my touch, leaning her entire body back. The momentum of gravity pulls at her hard, and I have to take a step toward her for more balance.

Except my shoe hits the same disastrous combo of weeds and slimy mud, and my balance dissipates. I fall toward her, and no matter how strong I am or how much I'd really, really love to save the girl, it's all for naught.

We both go crashing down, right into the chilly April waters of Podden's pond.

Calliope shrieks when she hits the water, and my breath is knocked clean out of me as I feel the iciness next. We both go under. Slimy ribbons of pond scum lap at my face, but I refuse to let go of Calliope. She's a strong swimmer, as am I, but no way am I letting her go.

We both fully submerge into the shallow water. Broken sticks and what feels like a rotten log hit my legs, and then I'm pulling her up to fresh air.

The water's not deep enough to be a bother, and we both come up sputtering in a sitting position on the mushy pond floor, water up to our shoulders.

Calliope uses her free hand to push sopping wet hair from her face, dead leaves snagged in and hanging from the ends. I give my head a hard shake and drag my free hand over my face.

We stare agog at each other, both shocked into silence, the argument forgotten.

I watch as a thin rivulet of pond mud slithers from her scalp down her temple, and I'm enchanted by the water droplets suspended from her eyelashes.

She stares at me in complete disbelief.

"You look like a fairy sea princess," I tell her truthfully.

She blinks, waterdrops fall.

I can't help it... I start laughing.

Immediately, I snap my mouth shut and bite down hard on my tongue. "I'm sorry."

Calliope blinks again and then her lips part.

I snicker.

Then snort.

Her beautiful eyes narrow on me, and the next thing I know, she's sending a wave of nasty pond water right at me. It catches me full in the face, hits the back of my throat, and I choke on it. I deserve it.

When I clear my eyes, Calliope is bent over, laughing hysterically, her shoulder dipping down into the water. The sound of her lilting voice is music to my ears, and I don't want it to stop.

So what's a guy to do?

I splash a wall of water back at her. She sputters and looks stunned for only a moment before her palms slap at the pond's surface, and I'm caught full in the face again.

Then it's on.

We both go at each other, laughing and splashing. Calliope comes up to her knees. She wobbles in the sucking mud but gets better leverage on me. I'm entirely doused by wave after wave. I hold up my arms, trying to protect myself, and suddenly realize I need to go more on the offensive.

I lurch up, lunge at her, and grab her wrists to stop the inundation. She's laughing so hard she barely has any strength left to fight against me. Her face is flushed despite the chill, and I can't fucking help myself.

I crash my mouth down on hers, feel her freeze in shock for a moment, and then gobble down the sultry groan that warbles out of her. It heats me to my bones, and then we're clawing at each other.

Grabbing, fisting clothing, attacking each other with our mouths. My hands make their way back to her face, intent on holding her still so I can consume everything she has to offer.

The kiss is atomic, off-the-charts hot, and filled with so much emotion I don't know whether she's coming at me with hate or something else.

Doesn't matter.

I'm not stopping.

Then something comes over me...a calm that feels like a steadying hand. I slow myself, make an exploring and leisurely swipe of my tongue against hers, and she melts into my body. An arm around her waist, I pull both of us to a standing position, the water lapping at my lower legs. I haul her into me and kiss her with all the regret I've been carrying around in my soul for years—a sincere apology.

Calliope wraps one leg around mine and puts her hands on my shoulders as if she's trying to climb up my body. I help her along, putting my hands under her ass as I haul her up. Her legs wrap around my waist, and our mouths never break contact.

She shudders in my arms, over and over again, and it's like a drug. Every part of her vibrates, even her lips against mine, and it's intoxicating.

I jerk my head back and look at her with a question in my gaze. She stares back at me, eyes hot but teeth now chattering audibly.

"Fuck," I mutter, turning to the bank of the pond. "You're freezing."

"J-j-j-u-s-t a little," she stutters.

I walk two paces and lower her to the edge of the shore, where she gingerly finds purchase in the grass. She looks down at her feet. "M-m-m-y-y-y s-s-s-and-al."

Huh?

I look down and note that one of her shoes is missing. I'm spurred into action, pointing at her tailgate. "Get out of those clothes so we can at least wring the water out. I'll get your shoe."

Calliope's fingers start working at the buttons of her shirt, and for a moment, I'm lost. She's not looking at me, but at the buttons she's fumbling with, and I wait with my breath stuck in my lungs as the first two pop free.

Her head lifts, and she tilts it in question.

"Fuck," I mutter and turn away, going back down to my knees in the water so my hands can move along the silt at the bottom. I push through wet leaves, sticks, and God knows what other kind of crud has settled at the bottom. As I move along, finding my Cinderella's lost shoe seems hopeless, but then I catch hold of the smooth, leather band. I didn't pay much attention to them before, but when I pull it out of the mud with a squelching sound and plenty of suction, I note regretfully that it's probably ruined.

I turn to her and hold up the hidden treasure I located for her, only to find her bent over and shimmying out of her wet jeans. A lacy thong and a shapely ass are revealed, curves that I know all too well. My body reacts despite the cold water and my own wet jeans, my cock starting to thicken at the sight of her.

She finally gets them off and is almost naked save for the thong and a matching lace bra. She turns toward me, and I'm not quite sure what my face reveals, but her chattering teeth stop, and she flushes from her cheeks down to the rounded globes of her breasts.

"Don't look at me like that," I warn her, taking a step out of the mud toward the bank.

"Like what?" she asks, and…yeah, she's not cold now. Heat and challenge are clear in her voice.

I don't bother answering her. It's rhetorical anyway.

When my foot hits the bank, I drop her sandal to the grass and immediately pull my wet T-shirt over my head.

Because you know…I need to wring it out, too.

Except I drop it to the ground, and it hits with a wet splat.

We stare at each other, each silently demanding something of the other. Are we on the same page? Does she want me the way I want her?

My silent question is answered when her trembling hands move to the center clasp of her bra, and with practiced ease, she flicks it open. The wet lace clings to her skin, so she has to peel it away. Her breasts spring free, nipples pebbled hard. I groan.

"You're beautiful, Poppy."

She doesn't chastise me again for using the nickname that was solely mine to use for her. Instead, with a bold look of determination, her thumbs go to the band on her thong, and she bends forward to inch the lace down her golden thighs.

I think I may have died and gone to heaven as her breasts sway with the motion. She steps out of the thong with such delicate grace that I'm mesmerized. My gaze narrows and focuses on the apex of her thighs. Trim, dark curls wet from the water glisten, and I hope what's nestled deeper is just as wet.

I move toward her with purpose, one hand going to her neck to hold her in place for my mouth, the other going straight to a plump breast.

Calliope groans and arches her damp body into me. My cock starts to ache with need.

Our kiss turns instantly ravenous, no more hesitant exploring and getting reacquainted. Everything I ever knew about this woman immediately feels like a comforting blanket. I trace the curve of her breast, flicking her nipple with my thumb.

"Rafe," she moans into my mouth as her hand latches on to my wrist. She pushes my hand down so it glides over her belly and moves right between her thighs.

She is no different than the woman I knew eight years ago. One of the things I loved most about her was that she could be demanding and never hesitated to let me know exactly what she wanted.

My fingers play with the lips of her sex, then find the warm, wet entrance and dip inside. With a feral growl, Calliope bites down hard on my lower lip. Suddenly, my jeans are way too tight.

It's a good thing she's feeling greedy because, in mere moments, her hands free my cock. I don't bother to wonder at her dexterity as she makes short work of my zipper and pushes the wet material down over my hips just enough so she can take my length into her palm. I hiss as she grips me hard and starts to stroke. And because I can give as good as I get, I press two fingers into her pussy and stroke that sweet spot deep inside.

That's all it takes before she's climbed back up my body, maneuvering up so high that her arms press down into my shoulders so she can angle herself above me. I spin to the edge of her Pathfinder and set my naked ass on it. Planting my feet hard against the ground, I brace myself as Calliope takes my cock in hand and starts to guide it to her entrance.

The first touch of her heat against the head of my dick is nirvana, and my hips strain upward for more contact. Her knees move to the cargo platform and she balances herself with her hands on my shoulders as she works her way onto my cock. I look down in fascination as I start to disappear into her, my head fuzzy, and my blood pounding in my ears. I glance up, see the look of fierce determination in her eyes, and fall a little bit in love with her again as her tongue peeks out from between her teeth in concentration.

Slowly, she lowers herself onto me, my one-time true heartmate and the sexiest lover I've ever had. She grinds all the way down as a tiny huff of exultant air escapes her mouth and blows across my face.

When she bottoms out, her forehead comes to rest against mine, and she holds utterly still for a painful moment.

My cock pulses inside of her, straining for release. I'm dizzy with lust and the need to flip her over and fuck her hard.

But I know one thing.

This is all Calliope right now. She has to set the boundaries of what we are. I need to let her be in control. Even if she were to climb off my lap and proclaim this to be a mistake, I would let her do so without an ounce of regret.

That's how grateful I am that she trusts me enough to let me back in.

Calliope sucks in a deep lungful of air, and when she lets it out, her mouth is back on mine. Her body starts to move, and she rises and falls on me.

She's so warm and tight, my nuts feel like they're going to implode. She fucks me slowly and with a tenderness that crushes my heart, knowing how difficult it must be for her to give that to the man who destroyed her.

My arms band around her tightly, and I kiss her with reverence. Tiny little moans slither out of her, and her movements become hurried...frantic. I want to hold back, let this play out for hours if possible, but I can feel the rush of an orgasm straining to break free. All those years disappear as I remember all the signals that indicate that Calliope is as close as I am.

The panting breaths, the yearning sounds deep in her chest. My hands move to her hips, and I help her in her quest to get to the same place as me. I pick her up, slam her back down so she feels me deeply.

Calliope grunts, bites down hard on her lip, and starts to bounce. My cock swells, my balls drawing inward as I feel that first ripple of pleasure through her pussy. Grabbing onto my shaft and sucking me in deep, I let loose with a hoarse cry of release.

She grinds down on me, hard, her entire body shuddering with her orgasm, her head falling back. I watch her with awe as pleasure ripples across her beautiful face, and her body quakes beneath my hands.

In this moment, I am validated, knowing that I never stopped loving Calliope.

Only now, I know I love her more than I ever did.

Chapter 8

Calliope

I step into my apartment and close the door, leaning heavily against it. My head tips back, resting against the hollow wood, and I sigh.

What in the hell possessed me to climb Rafe and have sex with him?

Sure, I could reason that it's been an emotional time for both of us since he got back—him with his dad, and me, well...being conflicted about him being back in my life.

I could say that I was addled by the cold dunk in Podden's pond and was overcome with a fit of the sillies. I've always been slightly impetuous.

Or maybe...just maybe...there's something still there between us that can't be reasoned or explained.

I'm not going to lie. It helped to hear Rafe's explanation of what happened back then.

I mean, it was a stupid explanation. About as dumb as a man can get, making decisions for his woman without any type of discussion. But there is something to be said for the fact that we were young—both barely eighteen. Even though it was entirely demeaning for him to make that decision on his own, I can't deny that it came from a place of love.

He'd said he was just as devastated by his decision, but the real question remains...can I believe it?

Another sigh, and I push away from the door. I need a shower and a cup of hot tea to think on this further.

I move through my small but entirely cozy apartment that I've lovingly decorated and filled over the years with homey items that make it uniquely my own. Soft alpaca pillows on my couch, a goofy painting of a cow wearing a red toboggan on his head over my mantel, and Yankee candles in every room, ready to lend mood-enhancing scents whenever I want.

My shower is delightful and long, and I wash my hair three times to make sure it's free of pond scum. I shave my legs, horrified they were slightly stubbly while having sex with Rafe, but also figuring he's felt my stubbly legs before. He used to tease me about it if I forgot to shave. I dry my hair, taking the time to blow it out, which means it will be styled perfectly tomorrow after I sleep on it. My thick hair always looks best on day two after a good shampoo. I slather lotion on my body, dress in a pair of comfy yoga pants and an off-the-shoulder T-shirt that's so well worn it's transparent in some spots, and move to the kitchen to make some strawberry hibiscus tea.

With steaming cup in hand and a few shortbread cookies on a paper towel to accompany it, I settle onto the couch to fire up my Kindle. Maybe getting immersed in a good book will help take my mind off my problems.

Mainly, how a gorgeous hockey star rocked my world a bit earlier, and how I don't even know how to deal with it.

I flip through my *to-be-read* list, purposely staying away from romances. I don't want anything to potentially make me swoon with possibility.

A knock on my apartment door startles me, but I swing my legs off my couch, figuring it's probably Mrs. Filmore from next door, bringing over some new baked goods recipe she's tried out. Her husband died last year, and she moved into the apartment next to mine, wanting to downsize and be closer to her daughter and grandkids, who actually live not too far from my parents' house.

I swing open the door, eager to see Mrs. Filmore because she's an excellent baker, but am stunned stupid when I see Rafe standing there with two grocery bags in hand.

I left him at his parents' house not more than an hour and a half ago. There was no kiss goodbye, only a promise to call me later. I didn't know what to—or if I should—read into that. The kiss would have implied some lingering affection; the lack of implying the sex was a one-time-only thing, and perhaps a mistake. Yet the promise to call spoke to wanting to see me again. Or maybe we'd just go back to being tentative friends.

Ugh. So confusing. In the moment, the only thing I can think to say is, "What are you doing here?"

"I missed you, too," he replies with a sly grin, pushing his way into my apartment.

"Why don't you come on in?" I mutter sarcastically and close the door, noting how good he smells as he passes me. "But, seriously...why are you here?"

Rafe takes a moment to survey my small apartment and then moves into the kitchen. He holds up the grocery bags. "I thought we could hang. I brought all the makings for tacos, and we can watch movies or something. Really great apartment, by the way. It's totally you."

I pad across the small living area and rest my forearms on the counter that separates it from the kitchen. He starts unloading the bags—ground beef, lettuce, tomatoes, a six-pack of beer.

"Dad's sleeping, and Mom's doing some spring cleaning," he explains as he moves to put the items in my fridge. "She shooed me out of the house, and I thought we could hang."

"Hang?" I ask skeptically. What does that even mean?

And then it dawns on me.

"Oh," I drawl in amusement. "You want sex again?"

Rafe pops straight up, looking at me over the refrigerator door, his eyebrows raised in surprise. "You offering?"

"Um," I reply, unsure of myself.

He grins at me. "As much as you totally rocked my world today at the pond, Poppy, I really just thought we could hang out. Get to know each other again."

My eyebrows draw inward, and I'm more confused now than ever. I rocked his world? Really?

Why I flush with pride is beyond me, but what makes a girl feel good is what makes a girl feel good.

Rafe shuts the fridge and moves around the kitchen counter to me. He takes my hand in his, covers it with his other, and brings them to his chest, his expression somber. "I know I can't possibly hope for you to understand what I did to you eight years ago, and I know it's likely a lot of wishful thinking that you could forgive me completely. But right now, we reconnected, and I want to see where this goes. Today with you has been the best day since I found out about my dad. I guess I just want more of it."

I'm drowning in his eyes and in his words. He's saying all the right things, and yet I can't let go of the feeling that drowning equals danger. He hurt me so badly before, and I know how easy it would be to fall for him again. I also know how quickly he could break my heart once more.

"You said you still care for me." He references the conversation we had at the pond while sitting in her vehicle. And I realize I do. I really do. I meant that.

"I'm scared, Rafe," I finally admit to him. "I don't think you'll ever understand what you did to me by leaving me behind without any explanation. Yes, you crushed me, but you also killed my self-esteem because I didn't know what I did wrong."

"You did nothing wrong," he assures me.

I nod. "Yes, you said that, and I believe you. But that doesn't negate all the work I had to do to build myself back up. I'm never going to put myself in a position again to be hurt like that. And, well...if you did it to me once, you could do it again."

Rafe's face crumples, not because I'm denying him something but because he feels like shit. I know him so well. I know when he feels awful about something, and I can tell he truly does. Making him feel bad wasn't my intent, but it's a bit of a balm to me right now that I think maybe he at least understands.

"But..." I continue because while he scares the shit out of me with the potential for more heartbreak, I can't deny that I'm happy to have him back in my life. I may have rocked his world at the pond today, but he turned mine upside down and inside out. I'm feeling all kinds of trampy right now that I want him again. "Maybe we can put some boundaries in place to help me feel a bit safer with you."

Rafe frowns, the implication heavy that he's a danger to me. "Like what?"

"We make it about sex only," I say with a slight shrug.

"Sex only, huh?"

"Well, yeah. I mean...that was pretty great at the pond, right? And it took your mind off your troubles. And I totally enjoyed the hell out of it, so we can have a sex-only relationship."

Rafe takes a step back and withdraws his hand from mine. "Yeah...that's not going to work for me."

I blink at him in surprise. "Why ever not?"

He scrubs a hand over his face in frustration and sighs. "Because I need your friendship, too, Poppy. You've helped me so much already with dealing with my dad. I mean, if I have to choose between friendship and sex, I would choose...and I feel like a total girl saying this, the friendship."

My lips quirk upward as my head tilts. "Well, of course, we can be friends, too. You know I love your dad, and I'm always going to be here to support him, you, and your mother. You have that."

Rafe's expression turns contemplative for a moment, his eyes shadowing skeptically. "So, let me get this straight... We're friends again, and we can have no-strings sex?"

"Friends with benefits," I reply with a brilliant smile. "It's a win-win situation for us both."

Rafe chuckles and shakes his head. He peers down at me, and for a moment, I think he might kiss me. Instead, he pivots to walk back into the kitchen. "You're a strange one, Calliope Ramirez. I guess it's why I adore you so much."

"You can't say things like that," I point out as he opens the refrigerator and pulls out two bottles of beer.

"Oh, right," he drawls with a sly look. "That might imply something deeper than just friends with benefits."

"Exactly," I reply pertly, accepting the beer he holds out to me. I twist the cap and give him an appraising look. "Want to have sex now or later?"

"Why now, of course," he replies seriously, setting his bottle of beer down on the counter. "Here? Bedroom? Couch? Floor? So many choices."

I giggle and set my beer down, too. "Let's start with the bedroom."

Chapter 9

Rafe

It's sort of like old times. Dinner at the Ramirez house. They invited my parents and me over, and Calliope is here, too, of course. I can't count the number of times throughout my childhood that we ate over here or they came to our house. The Ramirezes and the Simmonses were lifelong friends, their kids growing closer and closer as each year passed.

Tonight is the first time I've seen Mateo and Danielle Ramirez since I returned to Raleigh, though. Although I did see them infrequently over the years when I managed a quick visit to see my parents. They are as warm and welcoming as ever, not seeming to hold any grudges against me for breaking their daughter's heart eight years ago. Of course, I have no clue exactly what they know about the situation, but if I were a betting man, I'd say they know everything. Calliope is incredibly close to both her mom and dad and I expect they helped her pick up the pieces when I shattered her.

I also expect one of the reasons they might have put that all aside, making me feel welcome in their home right now, is because my dad is dying. Mateo is definitely the type of father that would take me aside and threaten to kick my ass for hurting his daughter, but he's also a good man. He's probably acting with some type of restraint, thinking that I'm facing a set of terrible circumstances right now.

Regardless, we have a great time. Danielle makes Mateo's favorite

Puerto Rican dish of *arroz con gandules* and fried plantains. Growing up, it was one of my favorites, too.

I know I'm not the only one who notices my dad picking at his food, not because he doesn't like it but because his appetite is at an all-time low. He seems frailer today than he did yesterday and the day before, and I wonder if there will be any good days left.

Still, he puts on a brave face, and there's a lot of laughter around the table as the rest of us scrape our plates clean.

It's been three days since Calliope and I reconnected at Podden's pond, and I'm not ashamed to say that she and I have been doing a whole lot more connecting since. The Cold Fury has been on break until the second round of the playoffs start tomorrow, and we take on the Boston Eagles, and I've been splitting my hours between spending time with my dad and hanging with Calliope. While she works at the hospital during the day, I attend team practices and meetings or sit by my dad's hospital bed as we play cards or watch TV. In the evenings after I eat dinner with my parents, I head over to Calliope's apartment.

She greets me with open arms, sometimes wearing nothing but some skimpy underwear which I definitely approve of. This is the new Calliope, a woman I'm getting to know all over again. Lingerie wasn't part of our teenage relationship. That was more about stolen moments when we could get them. But, fuck, I hate thinking about how she learned the art of seducing a man while wearing silk and lace.

I put that out of my mind, which is actually easy because when I'm near her, I'm consumed. To say that sex is different with her is an understatement. Again, it chafes at me hard to know that the things she now knows how to do with her mouth and her body she learned somewhere other than with me. And while Calliope was always forward and adventurous during our young, immature sex life, now she's openly wanton, and it turns me on more than anything ever has in my life.

Just last night, there was a note on her apartment door when I arrived that said simply: *I'm in the bedroom.*

What I found in there about had me exploding in my pants.

Let's just say that Calliope, naked in the middle of her bed, pleasuring herself with a vibrator had me seeing stars. I just stood there, transfixed as she brought herself closer and closer to orgasm. While her eyes were closed as she rolled and gyrated on the bed, that little pink toy between her legs, she knew I was there the entire time. She put on a show for me that drove me fucking nuts, and before I knew it, I was on her.

The toy was flung aside, and my mouth was pressed to her pussy, lapping and sucking at her until she exploded against me with her hands fisted tightly in my hair so she could grind against my face. It was fucking erotic as hell, and when she came down from her high, she looked at me with amazement. "You've learned a few things too over the years."

Fuck if that didn't rub me raw, too. The fact that we didn't learn the pleasures of oral sex together.

"So, Rafe," Mateo says as he picks up his glass of wine and takes a sip. "How does it feel to be playing for the Cold Fury now?"

"Honestly," I tell him with an easy smile, "it wasn't a hard adjustment. All the guys on the team are great, and it's been a seamless transition."

"You played well in your first games," he compliments me.

"He should be on the first line," my dad grumbles, and even though that's not exactly true, it fills me with a rush of love that my dad has become my most fervent fan. I know he feels like he's making up for lost time, and I need to let him know how much his words mean to me. But that's a conversation for later while in private.

Mateo and my dad start talking about the playoffs, while Danielle and my mom discuss planting their spring flowers. They're both passionate about gardening.

Picking up my wineglass, I sneak a glance across the table at Calliope, who sits directly opposite me beside my mom. Her return look is transparent and makes my blood heat. She's counting down the minutes until dinner is over, and she and I can be alone together.

"Are you and Calliope back together again?" Mateo asks me, and I'm so startled by the question that I choke on the wine I just took a sip of.

My eyes slam into Mateo's, and I see the overprotective father I'd been wondering about. I know just how easy he was taking it on me.

His expression is clear, filled with both wonder and suspicion. Will I hurt his little girl again?

I risk a glance at Calliope, and she stares back at me like a deer caught in headlights. We've not said a thing to our parents about our sexual affair, although my mom knows full well that I've been going to Calliope's in the evenings. I mean, I couldn't lie to her when she asked where I was going that first night after Podden's pond, but she thinks it's just a newly forming friendship.

At least, I think.

"Papa," Calliope simpers as she looks at her father, sitting at the head of the table to her left. "Why would you ask such a thing?"

"Because it's obvious there's something going on between you two," Mateo retorts with a knowing look at his daughter.

"You've been going over to Calliope's in the evenings," my mother points out, and my return glare calls her out for the traitor she is. She merely smiles sweetly back at me.

"And you two haven't stopped stealing glances at each other all evening," Danielle remarks with a sly grin.

"And you've been in an extraordinarily good mood the last few days," my dad chimes in.

Calliope ducks her head, hiding an amused smile.

I merely take my napkin and wipe at my lips, stalling for time as I collect my thoughts. I need to tread carefully here, so as not to get any parent's hopes up that we're back together in a normal relationship. I don't want to poke at Mateo's ire either.

Finally, I say neutrally, "We've rekindled our friendship. Calliope has been a great support to me since I returned home."

I glance around the table. Not one of our parents seem to be buying that lame statement. My dad actually snorts.

"She's been invaluable in explaining the medical details of Dad's condition," I assert, knowing in my heart of hearts that sounds even lamer. But I can't stop now. "She's a good friend. A childhood acquaintance. Those ties remained strong throughout the years, and—"

"We're friends with benefits now," Calliope says, and my entire body flushes hot as my eyes snap over to Mateo, prepared for him to spring across the table and lunge at me. His eyes rest heavy and hard upon me, and I flush hotter.

"Calliope Colleen Ramirez," Danielle exclaims, clearly mortified by her daughter's outburst.

I turn my gaze slowly to Calliope, giving her a death glare. She reaches out and pats her dad's arm. "It's fine, Papa. Your little girl—who is, in fact, a woman now and doesn't need protecting—knows exactly what she wants. Oh, and Rafe was also telling the truth...we are indeed friends, and I'm here to support him in any way I can."

God, the way she supported me last night with my balls heavy in her hands—

I shake my head, clearing those thoughts because I'm apparently way more transparent than I gave myself credit for this evening.

"Well, I for one think it's lovely that the two of you have"—my mom struggles to find the right words and then brightens—"rekindled your friendship. You two have a lot of years of history between you, and it makes me happy."

"Me, too," my dad says with a firm nod. "I'm glad Rafe will have someone to lean on when I'm gone."

And just like that, the mood turns from awkward and weird to somber. The silence around the table is heavy, thick with a gravity that's hard to dispel.

But, to my surprise, it's Mateo who saves the day. Who takes the gentleman's way out when he could have easily throttled me. He holds up his wine glass. "I propose a toast."

No one moves for a second, and then slowly, other wine glasses are raised.

Mateo looks straight at me. "Here's to friendship. Among all of us. To my extended neighborhood family—and in particular, to Calliope and Rafe—may they find exactly what they're looking for while on this new path."

I nod at Mateo and reach my glass to the middle of the table, where we all clink in acknowledgment of the toast.

My eyes move to Calliope, her gaze shimmering with mischief as she stares back at me. Well, at least it's all out in the open now.

I guess there's that.

Chapter 10

Calliope

I've been to Houlihan's numerous times over my life, many times with my family, a few times when Rafe and I were dating, but never on a game night. Since the Cold Fury franchise came to Raleigh in 1997 when I was just four years old, they set up Houlihan's as their hangout since it's right across the street from the arena.

There is a large segment of fans that don't bother going to the games but instead come to Houlihan's where they camp out at the bar and dinner tables, knowing that many of the players come to hang out after the game.

Over the years, it's become a tradition, and the players rub elbows and mix with the commoners. It's supposedly quite a treat, but it's also a packed madhouse, so you need to be prepared to wait forever to get a table, and if you're lucky enough to land that, then you have to wait forever to be served your food and drink.

Mostly, it's just people elbow to elbow, standing around, drinking beers and munching on chicken wings, waiting for the team to come in after a glorious five-to-two victory over the Boston Eagles to take game two of the second round of the playoffs. The atmosphere is electric, the mood jubilant.

I check my phone and see a text from Rafe. *Be there in five minutes.*

I have to wonder what I'm doing here. Not just in Houlihan's, waiting to meet Rafe after he played an amazing game, racking up two assists. But here in general, at Rafe's request to watch the game and then join him after at Houlihan's so he can, as he put it, "introduce me to the team."

That smacks of relationship to me. Says he wants me to be at the game to cheer him on, and he wants his new mates to get to know me. It goes far beyond the boundaries I laid out regarding how this would be a relationship focused foremost on sex and would not move into any questionable type of intimacy.

In fact, I had mentioned that to Rafe when he handed me the ticket he'd bought for me and said, "I'd really love for you to come to the game."

"But why?" I asked, actually confused. It happened to be my day off, and he'd stayed all night. When the subject came up, he was in the process of pulling on his pants, wanting to get home to have breakfast with his mom and dad before he headed off to the arena for a light morning skate.

"Because," he said simply, "I want you there."

"This is just sex," I pointed out, sitting in bed and bringing the sheets up over my naked breasts. He'd just finished thoroughly wrecking my body with a morning quickie.

Rafe spun on me, his eyes flashing with…something. Anger? Amusement?

I couldn't tell because he was back on me, and I was under him, pinned to the mattress. His face hovered, blocking out everything as he leveled me with a feral smile. "That's not true, Poppy."

"Is so," I whispered.

Rafe shook his head. "No. You said we were friends with benefits. The benefit is sex, I'll give you that. But we're friends first and foremost. That comes before the sex. It always has, and as my friend, I'd like you to come to the game tonight. And after the game, assuming we win— which I know we will—I want you to come to Houlihan's to meet my teammates."

"But—"

He kissed me to shut me up. It worked, and I got distracted, but then he pulled back and rolled off the bed. Snagging his shirt and shoes from the floor, he moved to my door and threw one last look at me. God he was so gorgeous with his hair tousled and day-old stubble on his face. "Come as my friend, Calliope. But if you don't, then I'll get the message. It really is just sex and nothing more."

Man, those words had punched into me hard, leaving me so breathless I couldn't even respond. Didn't matter...he left, taking away any opportunity to even argue with him.

And now here I am.

I totally enjoyed myself at the game. By mere virtue of knowing Rafe my entire life and watching him play hockey for most of it, I'm a true fan. Dedicated to the Cold Fury, who have been a staple in our household since I was a small kid. Rafe and I used to watch them together on the TV with our dads, and on the rare occasion we'd get a treat...tickets to an actual game.

I would admit to no one how excited I was when Rafe got his first assist. It felt like a victory for me. I wanted to scream at the top of my lungs... *"That's my friend out there on the ice!"*

My lover.

Used to be the love of my life. My best friend.

But now...just a friend that I have sex with.

I realize how ridiculous that all sounds, but really, I'm just protecting myself. We can phrase it however we want, and we can put it in a pretty package with a bow and call it a friends with benefits deal. But when it boils down to it, I'm merely protecting my heart from Rafe. I don't want it to be broken again.

If you're protecting yourself, then why the hell are you even here? Why are you letting him draw you back into his world?

I have no answers, only that I want to be here, and I fully believe that I'm merely being a good friend by doing so.

I move farther into the crowd, trying to make my way to the bar, but it doesn't take me long to realize there's no room for purchase. People are packed in like sardines.

But then something happens. The noise level rises incrementally, and the crowd seems to swell and shift. Things loosen up, and I even spot a small path right through to the bar.

It's then that I realize the swell of people are actually moving like a tide toward the doors, and it hits me then that some of the players must be coming in. I rise to my tiptoes, able to see nothing but the tops of the heads of the Cold Fury players. There's no way I'll be able to even get near Rafe with the throng of fans pressing in on them.

I pull out my phone and whip out a quick text to him. *I'm in the back of the restaurant near the restrooms.*

Once sent, I move that way, intent on waiting for Rafe to have time with his jubilant fans. I watch in amazement, wondering if he's used to this kind of fame and adoration. It's a life I would have led with him, but who knows if I would have ever gotten used to it. Right now, it seems alien and slightly scary, being at the center of such a huge spotlight.

I lean against the wall that separates the entrance to the alcove that holds the bathrooms and watch the celebration at Houlihan's play out. Then I sense the crowd seem to swell again, pushing outward and then miraculously splitting apart.

Suddenly, there's Rafe, eyes locked on me, walking purposely toward me. People try to get his attention for photos or an autograph, but for the moment, he ignores them all.

When he's ten feet away, he reaches a hand out to me, and I'm powerless not to reach back. Our fingers touch, and then they lace together. Rafe steps into me, lowers his head, and presses a kiss to my cheek. "Didn't want to leave you alone. Let me sign a few autographs, and then we'll get a drink."

"Okay," I murmur, completely thrown that he'd even bother to make me a priority right now. He's got fans to cater to.

As soon as I'm tucked into his side, he lifts his head and smiles openly at the first fan approaching. A woman—very pretty—standing with three of her girlfriends. She holds out a game program and a Sharpie, silently requesting an autograph.

Rafe signs her program, then her friends'. They gush and welcome him to the team.

"Can we get a picture with you?" one girl asks and hands her phone off to a fellow fan to take the picture.

"Sure," he replies easily and moves to stand in between them. Two women flock to each side, and he puts his arms around them, giving a wide smile as they get their picture taken.

People start to swarm, moving in front of me, wanting to be next in line to get Rafe's attention. He sees it happen and immediately jumps into action.

Pulling away from the women he was taking a photo with, he shakes his head and chastises the crowd. "Hey...hey...she's with me. Don't push her back."

Everyone freezes, and then Rafe is once again reaching for me, his hand locking tight on mine. Once again, I'm by his side, and he resumes catering to the fans.

A mere forty minutes later, he has me at the end of the bar and is buying us beers. The furor has died down, most of the fans now back in their groups, drinking and celebrating.

A couple joins us, and Rafe introduces me to Garrett Samuelson, one of the best players in the league.

After we shake hands, Garrett introduces me to the beautiful blonde at his side. "This is my wife, Olivia."

We barely get our own handshakes and pleasantries completed when more of the Cold Fury team starts to crowd in around us. It's a bit overwhelming, meeting these stars that I watch on TV, and it's utterly surreal that they treat me like the closest of friends because I'm here with Rafe. It's clear by some of the knowing looks that I get that Rafe may have told them something about the history of our relationship, or at the very least that we are lifelong friends.

Regardless, I'm about to lose my shit when the crowd parts again and the incredibly beautiful and insanely intelligent general manager of the Cold Fury, Gray Brannon, starts walking our way. Beside her is one of the best goalies of all time, her husband, Ryker Evans. He retired about a year and a half ago from the Cold Fury, and he's now the goalie coach for the team.

Talk about hockey royalty.

Rafe is amused when I get tongue-tied during introductions, but I manage to compose myself when Gray asks me what I do for a living. We chat for several moments, and I forget she's the head of a dynasty. Ultimately, she pulls out her phone, and I get to see pictures of her son, Milo.

"You know," she says, leaning in to me. My eyes move over to Rafe, who's busy chatting up Zack Grantham, his second-line teammate. When I look back to Gray, she's got an understanding smile on her face. "I've heard through the grapevine that you've been an immense support to Rafe with everything he's going through."

"We've been friends for a long time," I tell her, just vague enough to keep things, well...vague.

"I heard there was a time you were a lot more," she replies. And, yeah...Rafe must have spilled the beans to some of his teammates.

I take stock of how that makes me feel, and I realize it doesn't make me feel anything one way or the other. It's the absolute truth. There was a time when we were everything to each other, and then we weren't. Rafe made a mistake and ended things, believing with a foolhardy nature that he knew what was best for me.

"We're just friends now," I hasten to reassure her.

"I think you're more than that," she replies with so much surety, I have to wonder if she has magical powers to see the future or something. I want with every fiber of my being to argue with her, but before I can, she continues on. "People make mistakes, and some deserve forgiveness. Others don't. That's up to you to decide. Regardless, I think it's remarkable that you can put that aside and be here for Rafe. You're the best type of friend a person could have."

And just like that, Gray is pulled off into another conversation, and I move over to Rafe. I try to join in on the banter he has going with Zack and his wife, Kate, but my mind won't stay on point. I keep thinking about Gray's words, trying to figure out if it was wise advice that I should listen to, or just chalk it up to her being a nosy busybody.

Except I have a pretty solid feeling that no one in their entire life has ever thought of or called Gray Brannon a busybody.

Chapter 11

Rafe

My phone vibrates in my pocket—the repetitive buzz that indicates an incoming call. I consider ignoring it, but I'm not doing anything I can't step away from for just a little bit. I mean, I'm just holding vigil over my dad while my mom is at the grocery store.

I left for Boston five days ago to play games three and four of the second round of the playoffs. We swept them easily, and while it was an excellent respite to be lost in the thrill of playoff competition, I felt like I was missing something big back here in Raleigh.

Sure enough, when I returned late last night, I found that my father had taken a nosedive. I knew this could happen.

Would happen at some point.

Calliope and her medical expertise have been invaluable to me. I'm one of those people who always does better if I know the full, cold, hard painful truth of things. I can deal as long as I know what I'm dealing with, and she hasn't held back on how bad it can be.

And yet, when I saw my father lying in that hospital bed in the living room, looking a million times frailer than when I left less than a week before, I knew everything had changed.

I knew my dad wouldn't be able to make it to any more games, and we'd be lucky if he could take meals at the kitchen table with us. I knew that my time with him was limited, and my hands were tied on game days and with travel. I realized there's a very real chance that I might be gone when he takes his last breath, and I'm still trying to figure out how to reconcile that.

I snap myself back to the present. I have no clue who is calling, but I could use a break. My dad's been sleeping deeply, aided by a few drops of morphine that I put under his tongue a bit ago. He refuses to ask for it, but I can tell by his shifting and grimacing that he's in pain, so I strongly encourage him to take it. It felt both weird and right to put my hand behind his head and gently lift it from the pillow so I could give him the medicine.

I snag my phone from my pocket, needing a break from the heavy feelings that seem to be pressing down on me at all times lately. The only respite from them is when I'm deep inside Calliope, but those times are limited by my travel and spending time with my dad.

Not even glancing at the screen to see who it is—because, at this point, it could be a telemarketer, and I'd welcome the break from my thoughts—I answer. "Hello?"

"Just checking in, dude." It's Aaron Wylde. He's been in contact with me nearly every day since I left Phoenix, either by call, text, or email.

"How are you doing?" he asks lightly. I appreciate the tone because he knows how bad it can get, and he doesn't want to bring me down right off the bat.

"I'm hanging in there, man," I murmur in a low tone, pushing up from the chair next to my dad's bed. I doubt he'll wake up, but I decide to move away in the off chance I might disturb his sleep. I think it's the only time he's genuinely comfortable right now.

I head into the kitchen and pull open the sliding door that leads out to the deck. It's a beautiful day, sunny and in the mid-seventies.

"You're looking really good in Cold Fury skates," he remarks, a pointed statement that indicates he's been watching, as I'm sure many of my teammates have. I got traded from a team that's heavily favored to make it to the championship round, to a team that won the last two Cups and is heavily favored to make a run at a third. It was a huge risk for the team to let me go, and while I know it was one man's decision—team owner, Dominik Carlson—I also know he asked some of the team to weigh in on the decision. He specifically asked the first-line players...the big guns, whether or not he should let me go so I could tend to my dying dad. They all unanimously agreed that it was the right thing, even though it could hurt them going forward in the playoffs.

Those are the truest types of friends, and I miss them greatly.

We chat for a bit about the playoffs. The Vengeance is heading into game five of their playoff round against the Vancouver Flash tomorrow night. They're playing hot, and there are small moments when I regret not being there. All I have to do is look back through the kitchen into the living room and see my father lying in that hospital bed to know that I'd give up a million Cup championships to be here with him right now.

"How's he doing?" Wylde finally gets around to asking.

"He's slipping a bit more every day," I tell him, rubbing my hand over my face. "He sleeps a lot. Taking more of the pain meds. I think he's done eating."

Wylde sighs into the phone. "I know it's hard, buddy. I'm going to give you some advice, okay?"

"Okay," I readily agree. He's already given quite a bit, mostly on how to manage hockey and a dying parent. How to keep focused and my head in the game, even though my thoughts are often scattered in a million different directions.

"If there's anything left that needs to be said," he says, giving a dramatic pause that makes my ears really tune in, "don't wait to say it. Don't let embarrassment or a lack of a foundation hold you back. Don't let yourself have any regrets."

I consider his words. I've never been one to have deep discussions with my dad, nor he with me. Our relationship these last few weeks since I've been back has been easygoing, as much as it can be with such a dark cloud hanging over us.

"My dad was a horrible drunk," Wylde tells me, and my body jolts from the proclamation. I didn't know a lot of the details, only that he had a parent die of cancer and went through many of the things I'm going through. "I hated him for the longest time. We didn't speak for years, and I was fine with that."

There's a long moment of silence, and I wonder if he regrets saying these things to me. But then he continues. "But when I found out he had stomach cancer and was dying, I had a really hard decision to make."

"To choose to let those feelings go?" I venture a guess.

"That was part of it," he admits. "I knew my time to do something was limited. I had to not only let my hatred go, I also had to figure out how to love him again in a very short period of time. And that meant I had to talk to him and really communicate my feelings."

"But I don't hate my dad." I may have had some bitter feelings over time that he wasn't there for me the way my mom was, but that wasn't important.

"You don't have to hate your dad to want to make things as right as you can for him so he can transition away from this life with peace."

His words slam into me so viciously, I almost double over from the pain. I wonder, is there anything that my dad needs from me to make it easier for him to let go?

"Just talk to him as much as you can, Rafe," Wylde says softly and with a wisdom that I can't discount. "Do whatever you can to ease his suffering, and I'm not talking about the physical side of things."

"Thanks, Aaron," I murmur, more than grateful for the advice. I'm not sure I would have figured that out on my own.

"I'm here for anything you need," he assures me. "You call anytime, day or night."

"I will," I promise, knowing that I'll take him up on that. He's the only friend I have that knows exactly what I'm feeling right now, and I'm not above taking advantage of that resource.

"How's the love-life going?" he asks me with a chuckle. The last time we talked, I filled him in on reconnecting with Calliope, including details of our sordid past. When you bare your soul about a dying parent, talking about your first love is pretty easy.

"It's complicated," I reply but don't offer any more. While Wylde is the best man to talk to about what I'm going through with my dad, he's absolutely clueless about love and relationships. He's, without a doubt, the resident playboy on the Vengeance team, and breaking hearts—not mending them—is his specialty.

"I'll give you the same advice," he replies, amusement evident in his tone. "Talk to her. Don't hold back. Tell her how you feel."

"She's not dying, though," I reply drolly, because talking to Calliope is probably harder than talking to my dad.

"She might not be," he says, and I can't help but smile at the amusement I hear in his voice, "but you don't want whatever is between you two to wither away because of lack of communication. Come on, dude...it's basic communication 101."

Much later, as I'm sitting by my father's bed while he continues to sleep, my mom in the kitchen making some sort of chicken casserole, I think about the things I want to say to Calliope. How I'd like to be able to make a go of things with her and put aside this ridiculous notion of hers that we can't be more than what we are.

But fear holds me back because I know, deep down, she hasn't forgiven me for what I did, and she thinks I'm going to do the same thing to her again.

She'd be wrong about that, though.

The question is, how to convince her of that? That's something I need to figure out.

Chapter 12

Calliope

I watch Rafe pick at his meal, worried over his lack of enthusiasm for Beasley's Chicken and Waffles. It was one of our favorite restaurants to go to together back in the day, and it was his suggestion to come here tonight. I'd stopped by the Simmonses' house after work and grabbed Rafe. His mom had texted me that she thought he needed to get away for a little bit, and I was happy to oblige.

A little too happy. I missed Rafe the five days he was gone in Boston. He called me when he had some free moments, and we texted regularly, but damn if that isn't starting to feel inadequate. It worries me to no end that I'm beginning to feel dependent on him for some of my happiness. That definitely breaches the boundaries I set.

Was this inevitable? Taking two former lovers who drifted apart and putting them back into an intimate situation. Feelings will grow, right?

It sounds stupid when I think about it in its simplest form. I also know my refusal to consider the possibilities with Rafe is rooted in fear. Which doesn't seem so stupid.

Still, I'm worried about Rafe—as I am about Brenda and Jim—and I can't hold back on him now, despite how concerned I am about the boundaries that seem to be disappearing. "Penny for your thoughts?"

He looks up, his fork stuck in the fried chicken breast sitting atop the waffle. "Sorry...what?"

He looks confused.

Lost.

"Looks like you got a lot on your mind. Want to share?"

For a moment, his face becomes etched with relief, and he even goes so far as to open his mouth to speak, looking as if he might spill his guts to me. I lean a little closer in anticipation.

Then, just as suddenly, his expression clouds, and he shakes his head. He even attempts a confident smile. "I'm good, actually. How about you? How's work going?"

No, no, no. This isn't good at all. He's withholding because he knows that anything he shares with me puts us into murkier water. Would he be sharing as my lover? My friend? The man who hurt me, and yet someone I've reopened myself to?

Would sharing mean something past friendship—which is surely hard to quantify?

"Rafe," I say gently, reaching across the table and taking his hand. "Seriously...how are you doing? Because I'm guessing not good, and I want to help."

"I'm good," he says, leaning back in his chair and crossing his arms over his chest.

My right eyebrow shoots up, the other one flattening. "Come on, Rafe...don't do this."

He stares back at me for a moment, his jaw working side to side as he contemplates me. He leans back even farther in his chair. "You want to know how I'm doing?"

I smile at him and prop my chin in my hand, ready to take on his burdens.

His gaze moves to the ceiling as he drawls. "Let's see..."

Attention back on me, he leans forward, crossing his arms on the edge of the table now as he gives me a pointed look. "Well, for starters, my dad is dying. Every day, he's slipping a little further away from me, and I'm running out of time. I have so much to talk to him about, but not enough time to do it in."

My expression turns sympathetic, and I give him an affirming nod, silently motioning for him to continue.

"And when I could be sitting beside his bed, soaking up those last minutes, I'm instead sitting here in a restaurant with a woman I love. And I'm too afraid to tell her that because it's against the fucking rules."

My chin jerks inward, and I straighten in my seat. When had his tone gone from bereaved to bitter?

Rafe pushes his plate aside and scoots his chair in closer to the table, which enables him to lean closer to me. "That's right. I love you, Calliope, and the mere fact that it's terrifying to admit that to you is fucked up beyond all measure. I remember the first time I told you. I was pushing you on the tire swing over at Kent Mitchell's house during one of his summer parties. I told you when your back was to me. I pushed you hard, you went flying away from me, and I let those words fly right along with you. The look you gave me over your shoulder as you came back was utterly stunned and joyous all at the same time. It was the look I expected because I knew it was the right time to tell you, and I knew you felt the same exact way about me."

I'm speechless, first and foremost by the memory he just painted so prettily. I remember that day as clearly as if it had happened yesterday, It was truly one of the best moments of my life.

"I love you," he says again, this time with his eyes laser-locked onto me. There's no way I can ever doubt how much he means it. "I've always loved you. Never stopped. All these years, it's only ever been you I loved. And I was recently told I shouldn't hold things like this back because one never knows how short on time you are. I don't want to go another minute without you knowing that you're the only woman I'll ever love, and this friends with benefits thing you cooked up is horseshit. I think you know that, too, Calliope."

My head moves left to right, then back and forth again, a silent denial of what he just said. "Rafe..."

He holds up his hand, indicating that he doesn't want to hear whatever I'm about to say based on the tone I just used while saying his name. "Calliope...if what you're about to say to me is anything other than that you love me in return, I honestly don't want to hear it. Because if you say anything other than that right now, it's only because you're too scared to do it, and I don't have time in my life right now to deal with those fears. I've got a lot more pressing shit on my plate."

A surge of anger courses through me that he'd actually refuse to listen to my thoughts, as scattered and incoherent as they would probably be because he has me so flustered.

But one thing is clear, and it's not fair that I'm being silenced. "I have a right to be wary, Rafe. Yes, we may have blurred some friendship lines, and things are totally complicated right now, but I have a right to feel this way."

"No," he says with an adamant shake of his head. "You don't."

I blink at him, totally shocked speechless.

He points his finger at me. "You *did* have the right to feel that way. For sure. You had the right to carry around anger and hurt feelings. I did you wrong, and I deserved your enmity. But not anymore. I told you why I did what I did. It was foolish and wrong and completely moronic. But I apologized for it. From the bottom of my heart. And no matter what you say, I know you've forgiven me. If you hadn't, there's no way you would have let me into your body. So now, we're in a position where you're just stuck, afraid to go forward, and clinging on to a past that's no more. It's a bad merry-go-round ride, and I'm getting off."

Once again, my chin pulls in, disbelief that this has all turned so sideways swamping me. "What are you saying?"

"I'm saying that I don't want to be friends with benefits anymore. I want a real, intimate relationship full of love and partnership with you. Hell, I almost believe my dad got sick as fate's way of getting you and me back together. And I'm saying I'll wait for you to realize this is meant to be. So when you're ready to move forward, I'll be here. But don't expect me to go backward to this farce of a situation where we fuck and pretend to be friends. That's not working for me anymore."

Half of me is appalled by his demands, but the other half is charmed. Still, I'm pissed. "You're giving me an ultimatum?"

"Yup," he replies with a confident nod.

Then he picks up his utensils and starts eating his food.

With gusto.

Clearly feeling better about his life.

Chapter 13

Rafe

Everything seems normal when I wake up. It's game day...the first game of the third round of the playoffs.

The conference finals, and we have home-ice advantage against the New York Vipers. My belly rumbles with nerves, but that's typical on any game day.

I quietly dress in my old bedroom. Long gone are the posters of Wayne Gretsky and Mario Lemieux, my mom having converted this into a guest room long ago. The bed is rustic wrought iron that squeaks with any movement, and the furniture is feminine. Not that it bothers me. It's merely a place to rest my body until my dad can move on. Until he does, I'm not going anywhere.

We have a team skate at ten a.m., but I want to get in a light workout—more stretching than anything—before, as my groin's been feeling a little tender after a fall I took last week on the ice. I'm not about to do anything to jeopardize my chances of playing because it's starting to become real.

The Cold Fury is on fire, and there's a real chance they—*we*—might win the championship for the third year in a row.

Grabbing my workout duffel, I open my bedroom door and tiptoe down the hall past my parents' bedroom. It's empty, of course. Mom has taken to sleeping on the recliner beside my dad in case he needs anything, though I'm not sure what that would be.

He slipped into unconsciousness over twenty-four hours ago, and we called the hospice nurse out. She checked his urine output—yes, I've become adept at emptying his catheter bag—and took his vitals. In a low voice, she told us it wouldn't be long.

I come out of the hallway and get my first glimpse of the living room. My dad is lying in the bed, the blanket pulled up to mid-chest. My mom is sound asleep in the recliner beside him, an old afghan draped over her shoulders. The dawning sun casts a yellow glow over the room, and I place my duffel quietly on the floor at the top of the staircase.

I move silently, not wanting to wake my mom up. It doesn't matter with Dad, as chances of him rousing are minimal. Nearing the bed, I note with a smile how peaceful my dad looks in his deep sleep, hopefully secured far away from the pain and torment of dying.

And then I notice how utterly peaceful he looks.

My heart thuds to a painful stop in my chest, and a wave of terror hits me. While I've been living every moment these last twenty-four hours knowing that death is imminent and could happen between one breath and the next, I'm not prepared for the reality of it.

I approach the bed hesitantly, my hand shaking as I reach toward my father. My eyes strain in the morning gloom to see if I can tell whether or not he's breathing. I press my palm against his face and then reel backward, away from the icy chill of his skin.

My father is dead.

There's no stopping the flood of tears that assault my eyes, and I do nothing but periodically blink to dispel them. They come in wave after wave, so I don't even bother wiping the wetness from my cheeks.

I take my dad's hand, curl my fingers around it, and rest my hip against the railing of the bed as I stare down at him.

Yes, he looks so very peaceful. There's even a slight smile playing on his lips, and I'd like to believe it means he was thinking of something happy in his last moments on this Earth.

I think of the conversation we had the day before yesterday, and now I'm the one who smiles.

Still crying, but smiling all the same.

I'd sat by his bed and, upon Wylde's advice, had a conversation with my father like no other.

"Dad," I'd said. "I just want you to know that I love you very much."

My dad blinked in surprise, and his eyes got emotional and wet. They were words I didn't give him very often because they were things we just didn't say a lot to each other. They were awkward and heavy, yet I didn't fumble over them at all. I spoke from the heart, wanting no regrets to weigh me down.

"I love you, son," he'd replied. "I wish we had more time together."

I took his hand, and it was all the encouragement he needed. His feelings came pouring out in a litany of love, fervent wishes, and wisdom for me to follow throughout my life. He apologized for not being a better dad, and I assured him that he was the best. He advised me to seek love and hold on to it hard, and I told him I was working on it. He knew I meant Calliope, and he merely nodded.

My dad got me to promise to always look after my mom, and even told me that he hoped she'd find love again one day.

Finally, he reminded me to live my life with honor, kindness, and integrity. We talked for forty minutes, a non-stop and welcome diatribe of parental advice from a dying man to his son, condensed down for time management.

Thinking about it now, I hope I never forget a word of what he said, or a minute of that time when I sat there holding his hand.

Before he nodded off to sleep, I told him something that I thought was necessary for him to understand. "Dad...Mom and I are going to be all right. I don't want you to worry about us. You need to move on from this life, knowing that we will survive, strong in your memory, and bound by your love. Don't hang on, Dad. Let go and be at peace."

And he had.

Blinking away the memory, I return to the present, not sure how long I stand there, clutching my dad's cold hand. He's not here anymore. Not really.

Eventually, I let it go and move to my mom's side. I squat by her chair and gently shake her by the shoulder. The minute her eyes open and land on mine, understanding filters in, and she starts to cry. I fold her in my arms and hold her for a very long time.

There's nothing but the two of us in our grief until I sense that it's not just the two of us anymore.

I pull back from my mom, who sniffles hard and looks over my shoulder as I straighten.

Calliope is standing there, her eyes pinned on my father. I didn't even hear the front door open.

Slowly, her gaze drags over to me, and her words stun me. "I just woke up and...felt that you needed me."

I take her in. She's in a pair of sweatpants and an oversized T-shirt, and her hair is a mess. Her feet are stuffed into unlaced tennis shoes, and it's clear she hurried out of her apartment.

Of course she felt like I needed her. Because I did. I *do*. It speaks to our bond, and no words are necessary to explain it.

Without hesitation, she moves past the foot of my dad's bed and launches herself into my arms. Calliope presses her face into my chest, and I can feel her body shake as she cries, mourning the loss of my father and perhaps expelling her grief for me as well.

She shifts, tipping her head back. "I'm so sorry he's gone, Rafe. And also...I love you very much."

Chapter 14

Rafe doesn't say, "*I love you*" back, but that's okay. I didn't expect him to.
Don't need him to.

Just like when he first told me he loved me while pushing me on the tire swing and he knew the truth of how I felt in return already. Like then, I'm confident in how he feels now. Even though it took me a few days to voice it to him—to work up the courage and the guts to admit my feelings aloud—I never once worried that he would waver or decide I wasn't worth waiting for. I had faith in him, still do, and that says a lot.

Currently, I'm sitting at the kitchen table, nursing a cup of tea while Rafe and Brenda sit by Jim's bed. I called the hospice nurse, and she came out to the house right away. As required by law, she verified that Jim did, in fact, pass on, and she made the call to the funeral home the family chose. She then collected the remaining narcotic pain medications—as also required by law—to dispose of them for the family.

Once she finishes, Brenda, Rafe, and I spend time talking quietly. Brenda and I hug frequently, and she cries most of the time. Periodically, Rafe slides his hand against mine until our fingers are laced, and that's enough for the moment.

The funeral home folks arrive. Brenda has to sign a bunch of paperwork, and I stand by Rafe's side as they discreetly place a blanket over Jim's body and move him to a gurney that will be placed directly in the hearse. Brenda, Rafe, and I follow them out of the house. We stand quietly on the porch, our arms around each other's waists, and watch as they load Jim up into the back of the funeral home's vehicle.

After they leave, there's no time to sit around. I make calls to my parents, and then I help Brenda make calls to their family members. Rafe calls his coach to tell him that he won't be there for the game tonight. It was a call the team had likely been expecting at some point, and I imagine there are plans in place to compensate. Jim had tried to get Rafe to promise him that he wouldn't miss a game no matter what, and Rafe had sternly but gently told his father that it wasn't his decision to make.

I know Rafe, though. There's no way he'd ever leave his mother's side on the day his father passed.

Eventually, Brenda moves off to her room to take a shower since we expect the house will start filling with well-wishers shortly. With that thought, I rush out of the house without even taking the time to put on a bra and tell Rafe I need to go back to my apartment to take a shower as well.

I promise to come back immediately.

He walks me to my car, our fingers laced. I can feel the gravity of the situation, and the hunch to his shoulders tells me all I need to know.

He opens the car door for me, and when I move to get in, he holds me back with a tug on my hand. My eyes move to his, and I note his head tilted as if he's curious about something. "Did you really feel something was wrong and that you needed to be here?"

I smile back at him. Over three hours ago, I had woken up in a panic, feeling an immense blanket of grief hit me. I'm not sure if I knew that Jim had died and that Rafe had found him, or if it was just an all-consuming need for me to be truthful with Rafe about how I really felt about him.

"I can't explain it. I just felt that it was urgent that I get here."

He nods, seeming to understand something that frankly seems implausible to me.

"And you love me?" he asks, his fingers tightening on mine.

I wondered when he'd finally address what I said to him. I'm not sure how much of a surprise it was, as he seemed pretty confident that I'd come around. He'd boldly told me he'd wait for me to come to the right conclusion, and well...here I am.

"I know the timing couldn't be worse," I say apologetically as I step in closer to him. "But yes...I do love you. I can't say I carried a torch for you all these years unless you count the type that I'd use to burn your house down, but I do know one thing...what you did was forgivable. I just had to accept that."

"So no more of this silly friends with benefits thing?" he presses, putting both palms on my hips.

My hands go to his shoulders, and I give him a sly smile. "I didn't say that. I mean, we are still friends—the best of—and there are many, many benefits between us. But I also know there is so much more."

I rise to my tiptoes and whisper before I kiss him, "So much more."

Rafe's eyes mist up, his mouth drawing down. His voice is heavy as he admits, "I'm so glad you're by my side right now. I miss my dad, and I'm not sure how to navigate this world without him in it."

"One step at a time," I assure him. "And I'll be right here along the way."

He murmurs words of promise to me—*I love you*—and then his mouth is on mine, giving me the most tender and binding kiss a woman could have the privilege of receiving.

"I love you," I assure him once again. I imagine I'll be saying it a lot because he needs to hear it, and well...so do I. They're the best words, after all, and they represent the good in our world. "We were given a second chance."

"I was given a second chance," he insists.

I shake my head. "No. We. My life wouldn't be complete without you. I wouldn't know a love like what you can give me. So, even though it took me a while to recognize it and not fear it, to accept it, it's my second chance, too."

Rafe pulls me in for a hug, and I squeeze him tight. His voice feathers over me. "Want to know one of the last things my dad said to me?"

I nod, my head pressed against his chest. My fingers dig into his shirt, and my eyes start leaking because I can feel the gravity in his tone.

"He told me he was leaving this Earth happy that you and I were back together. I mean...he didn't really know where we stood, but yet...somehow, he knew. I know it sounds crazy, but I can't shake the feeling that my dad's illness and death sort of fated you and me back together again. And while I'd give anything to have my dad back, I actually find it quite peaceful knowing I have you in his place."

And, of course, I start sobbing. I think I manage to say, "That's beautiful," but my face is pressed so hard into his shirt that I doubt he understands me.

Doesn't matter.

He just holds me tight as we both grieve our losses and marvel about our gains, both emotions seeming perfectly right.

Epilogue

Rafe

A lot can happen in four weeks.

A man can die.

A son can grieve his father.

A team can lose a championship.

A man can realize he'll love a woman for eternity.

James Carl Simmons was cremated, and his ashes now sit in my mom's bedroom. We have yet to have a memorial service, and that was at my mother's insistence. She wanted to get me through the rest of the playoffs, a matter she and my father decided behind my back and to which she stuck to her guns about. Within the next few weeks, we'll have an intimate gathering of family and our closest friends, but for now, Mom is fine having him close.

The Cold Fury fought a valiant battle, but in the end, we lost the war on ice. The Arizona Vengeance beat us for the Cup in game seven, and it was a bittersweet moment for me. I've become a full-blooded member of this Cold Fury team, and I'd die for any of my teammates. I wanted to bring that championship home so badly that I could taste it. Playing hockey and working for a team I believe in helped to take my mind off my grief.

And yet...a part of me is happy for my former Vengeance teammates. They deserve the win. They wanted it more. They outplayed us. The Cup is where it belongs, at least for this season.

Next season is another matter.

But for now, I am on official vacation for the next few months until training camp starts, and while my season has ended, my life is really just beginning.

"Okay," I warn Calliope playfully as I pull into the driveway. "No peeking."

"I won't," she grumbles, pulling down the dark scarf I tied over her eyes. "But, seriously...I have to pee, so I hope wherever it is you're taking me, we get there soon."

"We're here," I tell her as I put the car in park. "Don't move, though. I'll be right around to you."

Before she can reply, I turn off the engine and exit the vehicle, hustling around to the passenger door. I open it, take her by the hand, and gently help her out.

I carefully walk her toward the front of my car, making sure there's nothing for her to trip over, but it's only smooth concrete. I position her body and then place my hands on her shoulders from my place behind her.

"Okay...ready?"

Calliope nods, and I pull the blindfold from her face. I lean to the side so I can see her expression as she takes in the ginormous house in front of her. It's white brick with a sweeping front porch, shuttered windows, and almost fifty-six-hundred square feet of space that sits on its own private pond.

"What do you think?" I ask her, unable to hide the tinge of pride in my voice.

"It's gorgeous," she replies in awe as she takes it in. "Who lives here?"

"We do," I answer her simply, and it causes her to whip around and face me with disbelief. "I bought it. We can move in at any time."

Calliope's mouth drops open, and it's the perfect opportunity to kiss her. I do so without hesitation or regret and get lost in the way she kisses me back.

But all good things come to an end, and she pulls away, shaking her head. "Wait a minute...you bought a house. A beautiful mansion, and you want me to move in with you? Don't you think that's moving really fast?"

Oh, dear Calliope. You have no idea how fast I can move.

Without hesitation, or a moment's fear—and my mind flashing back to the beautiful girl I pushed on the tire swing and told boldly that I loved her—I pull the black velvet ring box out of my pocket.

Calliope's eyes bug out of her head.

I open it slowly...with a flourish, and I know she's not only dazzled by the moment but by the size of the diamond nestled inside. Four carats pack a whopping punch.

I sink to one knee, wincing slightly at the bite of concrete through my jeans. "Poppy...I love you so much, and there's been a lot of bad in my life lately. But finding you again...loving you again...has made everything infinitely better. There's no life without you in it, permanently by my side. So, please say you'll marry me, and that you'll move into this house with me, and that we'll have kids one day."

Calliope just stares agog at me, her eyes cutting from me to the ring to the house, then back to me again. "This is so fast," she mutters.

"No, it's not," I say firmly as I move to a standing position and take the ring from the box. I grab her hand, slide it easily onto her appropriate finger, and watch her as she stares down at it. "We've known each other for a lifetime. Loved each other for years. Made mistakes, fell apart, and found each other again. No one knows me the way you do, and no one will ever know you half as well as I do. And if there's anything I've learned over the last few weeks, it's to never live life on the verge of regret. We have nothing to lose. Let's do this, Poppy."

She touches the ring with the tips of her fingers, twisting it slightly. Then her head tips up, and she smiles at me. "Okay. Let's do this."

* * * *

Also from 1001 Dark Nights and Sawyer Bennett, discover Wicked Force, part of the Kristen Proby Crossover Collection.

Sign up for the 1001 Dark Nights Newsletter
and be entered to win a Tiffany Key necklace.

There's a contest every month!

Go to www.1001DarkNights.com to subscribe.

**As a bonus, all subscribers can download
FIVE FREE exclusive books!**

Discover 1001 Dark Nights Collection Seven

Go to www.1001DarkNights.com for more information.

THE BISHOP by Skye Warren
A Tanglewood Novella

TAKEN WITH YOU by Carrie Ann Ryan
A Fractured Connections Novella

DRAGON LOST by Donna Grant
A Dark Kings Novella

SEXY LOVE by Carly Phillips
A Sexy Series Novella

PROVOKE by Rachel Van Dyken
A Seaside Pictures Novella

RAFE by Sawyer Bennett
An Arizona Vengeance Novella

THE NAUGHTY PRINCESS by Claire Contreras
A Sexy Royals Novella

THE GRAVEYARD SHIFT by Darynda Jones
A Charley Davidson Novella

CHARMED by Lexi Blake
A Masters and Mercenaries Novella

SACRIFICE OF DARKNESS by Alexandra Ivy
A Guardians of Eternity Novella

THE QUEEN by Jen Armentrout
A Wicked Novella

BEGIN AGAIN by Jennifer Probst
A Stay Novella

VIXEN by Rebecca Zanetti
A Dark Protectors/Rebels Novella

SLASH by Laurelin Paige
A Slay Series Novella

THE DEAD HEAT OF SUMMER by Heather Graham
A Krewe of Hunters Novella

WILD FIRE by Kristen Ashley
A Chaos Novella

MORE THAN PROTECT YOU by Shayla Black
A More Than Words Novella

LOVE SONG by Kylie Scott
A Stage Dive Novella

CHERISH ME by J. Kenner
A Stark Ever After Novella

SHINE WITH ME by Kristen Proby
A With Me in Seattle Novella

And new from Blue Box Press:

TEASE ME by J. Kenner
A Stark International Novel

Discover More Sawyer Bennett

Wicked Force: A Wicked Horse Vegas/Big Sky Novella
By Sawyer Bennett

Kynan McGrath has just joined The Jameson Group, a security organization handling everything from covert military operations to providing protection for high-profile celebrity clients. As second-in-command, Kynan has the authority to accept or decline any mission. But when a stunningly beautiful pop princess walks through the doors, Kynan knows he'll do anything to get closer to her.

Joslyn Meyers is on the brink of super stardom, but with fame comes a level of attention she was never prepared for. She's even less prepared for the gorgeous, tattooed, British bodyguard her mom has hired to keep her safe.

When Kynan escorts Joslyn to her hometown of Cunningham Falls for a benefit concert, it becomes clear that the threat to Joslyn's heart is more real than any physical threat to her safety. But when Hollywood comes calling, will the pop princess and the wickedly hot Brit be able to preserve their relationship? Or will the force of their differing worlds drive them apart?

Wylde: An Arizona Vengeance Novel

By Sawyer Bennett

Coming May 12, 2020

There's a reason they call me Wylde and it's not just because it's my last name.

I might be one of the newest players on the Arizona Vengeance team, but I'm no stranger to the celebrity that goes along with being a professional hockey player. Whether it's a fan seeking an autograph or a puck bunny looking for more, I've grown used to the attention. I not only thrive on it; I use it to my advantage. Let's just say my bed is rarely empty.

When a quirky redhead at the local bookstore stops me dead in my tracks, I decide to pop in and turn on the trusty Wylde magic. As smart and strong-willed as she is beautiful, Clarke Webber isn't swayed by my witty banter or charming good looks. And when she realizes who I am and the fame that comes along with it, she likes me even less. Thankfully, I'm always up for a challenge. The more I get to know about her, the more I know my playboy days are behind me.

If I'm going to capture Clarke's heart, it's time to be a lot less Wylde, and a lot more Aaron.

* * * *

Chapter 1

Wylde

I love living in downtown Phoenix. My condo is on the fringe of the social scene, which is filled with trendy cafes, fine dining, and upscale shopping. At night, I merely have to step out of my building and walk one block west to be in the thick of it all. Five blocks south, and I'm at the arena where the Vengeance plays. My truck mostly stays parked in the underground garage unless I need to use it to drive to the airport for away games, but I'll often just Uber it.

I've always preferred city living, and I lived in downtown Dallas when I played hockey for the Mustangs before being traded to the Arizona Vengeance. It's a single man's playground, the city life, and I wouldn't trade it for one of those houses in the burbs that a lot of my teammates choose as their choice destination for fine living.

I ignore the elevator on the fourth floor of my building, choosing to take the staircase instead. For fuck's sake, I'm a professional athlete... I should be able to handle four flights of stairs coming and going.

When I step out into the June morning, it still takes me a moment to get past the startling dry heat. It seems like I'd be used to it since I've lived the last several years in the southwest between Dallas and Phoenix, but this New Englander still has a tough time living without humidity.

Regardless, today is the day I'd chosen to get back into the swing of things with my workouts and I can't let a little fire in the lungs before I even start my run stop me.

It was just ten days ago that my team, the Arizona Vengeance, won the Cup championship over the defending champions, the Carolina Cold Fury. It's been ten days of being lazy, eating bad food, and drinking lots of beer. I've been going out with my single buds on the team almost every night, getting drunk and heading home with a different puck bunny.

But fuck if I can only take so much of that type of hedonism. Like I said, I'm a professional athlete and with that comes a certain way of living.

For my entire hockey-playing life—starting before I was a teen—I took my training seriously. I'd been told by coaches early on I had raw talent, but part of developing that was in conditioning my body. That meant good nutrition, workouts, and maintaining a winning attitude at all times, even in the off season.

That's where we are now... the glorious off season of summer, but that doesn't mean I don't have to work.

Starting today, it's back on. Training camp is only three short months away, and the pressure for us to perform at the same or better standards is immense. On top of that, my contract expires at the end of next season, and I'll be damned if I'm going to operate at anything less than one hundred percent.

So today, I start back running and I usually average at least twenty miles a week, broken into four to five morning runs.

Many of my defense peers aren't into running, focusing instead on strength training and muscle endurance. Those are important to me, too, but I've always loved running for some reason. I'm easily able to let my head go into a subspace, and it's quite meditative for me. On top of that, it burns a lot of calories. It means I can eat more, which is a bonus given how much I love food.

I take a moment on the sidewalk to do some dynamic stretching—heel-to-toe stretches, hamstring curls, and leg kicks. I do two sets, walking up and down my condo's block, oblivious to the people who do double takes when they recognize me.

For the most part, that doesn't happen. Yes, I'm a well-known player for the Arizona Vengeance, a first-line defenseman, but the entire city isn't into hockey. More often than not, I'm able to go places without being recognized, but that's also dependent on where I go. Sports bars, I'm bound to get approached for autographs. The grocery store, less likely, particularly since I like to go early on Sunday mornings when it's practically dead.

Legs fully stretched, I start off in a slow jog heading east and after the first quarter mile, I pick up the pace. My ear buds are cranked, and DJ Khalil elevates me to run faster.

My mind wanders, trying to figure out my summer. I haven't given it a lot of thought as I'm more of an impulsive, do-things-when-I-feel-like-it kind of guy. I know I should plan a trip home to New Hampshire to see my mom, but the thought of it starts to depress and demotivate me, so I put it out of my head. We don't have the best relationship and any trips home are made from a sense of obligation, not because I actually get joy from our reunions.

That may seem harsh, but she'd say the same damn thing.

Normally, I'd plan a vacation on a sunny beach somewhere but in a few weeks, I'll be headed to the U.S. Virgin Islands to attend Brooke and Bishop's wedding. The entire team is going for a week to participate in a continued celebration of the Cup win in addition to their nuptials. It's going to be just one long party, and I'm looking forward to it.

Maybe I could head to Wyoming for a few days of fishing, something I got into over the last few years and really enjoy.

Or maybe I should go bum around Europe for a bit. I have several teammates who would be up for just such an adventure.

Regardless, anything I decide will have to wait until after Bishop and Brooke's wedding during the first week of July because my weekends are already accounted for until then.

Up ahead, I see they're doing some sidewalk construction on my normal route. At the next light, I decide to turn left. I jog in place while I wait for the light to change. As other mid-morning strollers casually jaunt over the crosswalk, I take off running again. Rush hour is over and most people are at their places of work, but I still have to weave in and out of other pedestrians.

This is a street I haven't been on. I pass a coffee shop, a small drugstore, and what looks like a bookshop.

I glance in the window of the latter, my gaze landing on an incredibly gorgeous woman behind the cash register. It's really just a glimpse as I run by, but her auburn-colored hair gathered in a messy bun on top of her head and the most stunning pair of eyes shining from under a pair of rectangular, black-framed glasses catches my attention.

Now, glasses aren't normally my thing on a woman, but, in this instance, they work. I can't tell if her eyes are green or blue, but they're light colored, in stark contrast against her fiery hair with tendrils escaping her updo and framing her pretty face.

And just as quickly as I spot her, she's gone because I'm past the bookstore and reaching the end of the block.

To return to my route, I should cut right and head uptown, but I can't shake that tiny glimpse of gorgeousness I just witnessed, so I decide to take another peek at the woman. I kick up my pace. Rather than turn around and go back, I decide to circle the block to get my paces in.

When I reach the bookstore and slow my pace to get a better look at the woman, disappointment sets in because she's no longer behind the register. I can't spot her anywhere. Granted, there's a lot going on inside the shop. It's more than just a bookstore as in addition to rows of books, there are tables and free-standing shelves that host a variety of knickknacks for sale. It looks cozy, interesting, and crowded at the same time, but there's no beautiful redhead.

And once again, the bookstore is behind me—the opportunity she represented now firmly in my rearview mirror.

I get to the end of the block, determined to turn right and get back on route. For some reason, though, I don't enter the crosswalk when the light turns green. Jogging in place, I peek over my shoulder at the bookstore, weighing my options.

"Fuck it," I mutter, pivoting and heading back that way.

Slowing to a walk a good ten yards from the door, I take deep breaths to get my heart rate into a normal range and cut the sound from my iPhone strapped onto my bicep. My breathing evens out quickly because, despite the ten days of gluttony and debauchery, I'm still in pretty great shape. I reach an arm up, wipe my sweaty brow on my sleeve, and take one last deep breath.

Pushing open the door to the bookstore, I note the name painted in gold letters—*Clarke's Corner*. A tinkling bell announces my arrival, and a husky voice calls out from somewhere behind the bookshelves.

"Be there in a moment."

"Take your time," I reply loud enough to carry, then proceed to browse around.

It's an incredibly cute place. All the furniture, including the four long rows of bookshelves that are jampacked with paperbacks and hardcover editions, are painted in a glossy white. The walls are done in a pale blue, covered with paintings by what look to be local artists. They must be commissioned for sale, because they have price tags. Tables are loaded with trinkets such as bookends, candlesticks, tiny lamps, gilded frames, and other useless objects used for decoration.

"Hi." That same voice hits my ears, but much closer, and I turn to find the beautiful woman I saw earlier there.

Without being too obvious, I take more of her in. She's wearing faded, worn jeans along with a pair of pink sandals. A gauzy, loose shirt of mint green hangs off one shoulder with a white tank underneath.

Her eyes are green, maybe hazel and now that I have a moment to observe, her glasses are actually tortoiseshell with gold trim around the edges. Surreptitiously, I note she isn't wearing a wedding ring. Actually, her hands are bare of any jewelry. Small gold studs wink in her ears behind the wisps of hair framing her face, which is classically beautiful without a single speck of makeup. Not even mascara or eyeshadow.

Just fresh, clean skin and clear eyes staring at me.

"Welcome to Clarke's Corner," she says brightly. "Can I help you find something?"

"Um…" I say, drawing an absolute blank. I can't very well say, *No, thank you… I came in here to hit on you because I found you absolutely beautiful as I was running by.*

I mean, I *could* say that.

And, actually, I have done that on occasion when I met a woman I was immensely attracted to. I'm no slouch in the looks department, so I've never found beating around the bush to be all that satisfying. More of the type of guy who goes for what he wants.

Then, it hits me. I throw a thumb over my shoulder toward the interior of the store. "Actually, I was walking by—"

"Kind of sweaty to just be walking by," she observes. "Are you sure you're okay? Do you need to sit down or anything?"

Sharp girl. And also one for honesty, it seems.

I grin, popping my panty-dropping dimples, holding my hands up in mock surrender. "Okay… got me. I was out running, and I'd never been this way before. When I saw this store, I remembered I have a wedding to go to this weekend and I haven't bought a present yet."

Total lie.

Well, sort of.

There is indeed a wedding. Erik, one of my teammates, is getting married to his fiancée, Blue, but I *have* already bought them a gift. I have no problem buying a second one, though.

"Did you have anything in mind, or would you like some suggestions?"

"I'll take suggestions," I say, leveling her with a sheepish but hopefully charming smile. "Not the best shopper."

The woman moves over to a wall unit that houses a few interesting pieces of pottery, then chooses a vase the color of burnt cinnamon with dark yellow swirling through it. "How about something like this?"

Taking it from her, I pretend to study it thoughtfully before I shake my head. "I don't think this is to their taste."

In truth, it very well could be. I'm not good at stuff like this, but if I accept the first thing she shows me, then the conversation is over and I'll have to leave.

She next shows me a pair of brass candlesticks. "Too formal," I say.

A porcelain picture frame. "Too feminine."

A music box. "Also too feminine."

Next up is a fancy wine opener. Well, that's actually a really good gift. Reluctantly, I nod with a smile. "It's perfect."

"Awesome," she replies, moving past me to get to the register. She smells of vanilla with an undertone of what might be oranges. It's pretty, and I can't quite remember the last time a woman's fragrance appealed to me.

"Would you like me to gift wrap this?" she asks.

"That would be awesome," I reply, because anything that will give me the opening I need to ask her out is all right with me.

I am most definitely asking her out.

I mean, she's hot, but she has this nerdy quality going on with the glasses and innocent fragrance. Her clothes are slightly baggy, not the form-fitting, bare-all concoctions most women I hook up with wear.

She's like a breath of fresh air and this perplexes me, because I've never been overly attracted to her type before.

"So how long have you been working here?" I ask genially as she reaches under a cabinet behind the register to pull out a long bin with wrapping paper in it.

"I own the place," she replies without looking up. In her tone, there's amusement I would never even consider she was the owner, along with pride in herself that she owns this place.

"Wow," I reply, surprised and impressed. I turn around, taking in the store once more. She must be doing okay since this is a high-rent commercial district of Phoenix.

"Opened it about six months ago," she replies, rummaging through the bin. "Lifelong dream and all."

"Good for you." I lean on the checkout counter, watching her with appreciation while her back is turned to me. "So, I take it you're the 'Clarke' of 'Clarke's Corner'?"

Without warning, she glances over her shoulder at me and I manage to tear my eyes off her ass just in time. "That's me. Clarke Webber."

"Aaron Wylde," I reply in turn. I watch carefully to see if there's a glimmer of recognition, since I *am* a famous hockey player, after all. But she didn't seem to recognize my face when I walked in, or, if she did, she played it super cool.

Now, she just gives me a polite nod and murmurs, "Nice to meet you."

Yeah... she has no clue who I am, which means she's not a hockey fan. It isn't all that surprising. While the Vengeance coming to Phoenix last year generated immense buzz and excitement, not everyone is a fan. I saw a recent article that said TV viewership for the final Cup championship game was at 2.9 million. Contrasted to the 19.3 million people who watched the *Game of Thrones* finale, it's obvious to see professional hockey is a niche.

Clarke jolts me from my thoughts by turning to face me.

"Is this a formal wedding or something a bit more casual?" She holds up two different rolls of paper. I'm assuming one is fancy and the other isn't, but fuck if I can tell the difference.

"It's going to be an outdoor wedding, so I'd say maybe casual."

"Got it," she replies, attention returning to the wine opener. As she works at removing the price tag and wrapping it, I prattle on, which is weird for me. "It's kind of a spontaneous type thing. The couple is engaged, and they were going to do something bigger, but they had an accidental pregnancy, so decided to just go for it."

"Oh, good for them," she intones, and I can feel the smile in her words. "And, honestly, if they already have a wine opener—and chances are they do—it's always good to have a backup."

With the package wrapped, she starts to ring up the purchase. A surge of panic hits me when I realize that, once this exchange is complete, I'll be expected to walk out that door with a wrapped wine opener under my arm—which I don't need—and this gorgeous woman but a memory.

I struggle to think of *anything* to get our conversation where I need it so I can make a move. Ask her out and arrange something.

Fuck, this is hard.

I suppose it comes with the territory of being nothing but a playboy who prefers to hop from bed to bed. Also, it's a bit of an issue that I often rely on my looks or fame to get me where I'm going. Most of my hookups happen after games or in bars where literally dozens of puck bunnies throw themselves at me and it's just a matter of choosing the one I'm most attracted to.

"What kind of books do you sell?" I blurt out.

Clarke blinks those dreamy eyes, her auburn brows drawing inward slightly as if that's the weirdest question for a bookstore owner to get. "Um… a bit of everything, really. And if I don't have what you're searching for, I can easily get it for you. Something in particular you need?"

And… another dead-end conversation.

I haven't read a book in years.

About Sawyer Bennett

Since the release of her debut contemporary romance novel, Off Sides, in January 2013, Sawyer Bennett has released multiple books, many of which have appeared on the *New York Times*, *USA Today* and *Wall Street Journal* bestseller lists.

A reformed trial lawyer from North Carolina, Sawyer uses real life experience to create relatable, sexy stories that appeal to a wide array of readers. From new adult to erotic contemporary romance, Sawyer writes something for just about everyone.

Sawyer likes her Bloody Marys strong, her martinis dirty, and her heroes a combination of the two. When not bringing fictional romance to life, Sawyer is a chauffeur, stylist, chef, maid, and personal assistant to a very active daughter, as well as full-time servant to her adorably naughty dogs. She believes in the good of others, and that a bad day can be cured with a great work-out, cake, or even better, both.

Sawyer also writes general and women's fiction under the pen name S. Bennett and sweet romance under the name Juliette Poe.

For more information visit https://sawyerbennett.com

For a complete list of books available from Sawyer Bennett, please visit: https://sawyerbennett.com/bookshop/

Discover 1001 Dark Nights

Go to www.1001DarkNights.com for more information.

COLLECTION ONE
FOREVER WICKED by Shayla Black
CRIMSON TWILIGHT by Heather Graham
CAPTURED IN SURRENDER by Liliana Hart
SILENT BITE: A SCANGUARDS WEDDING by Tina Folsom
DUNGEON GAMES by Lexi Blake
AZAGOTH by Larissa Ione
NEED YOU NOW by Lisa Renee Jones
SHOW ME, BABY by Cherise Sinclair
ROPED IN by Lorelei James
TEMPTED BY MIDNIGHT by Lara Adrian
THE FLAME by Christopher Rice
CARESS OF DARKNESS by Julie Kenner

COLLECTION TWO
WICKED WOLF by Carrie Ann Ryan
WHEN IRISH EYES ARE HAUNTING by Heather Graham
EASY WITH YOU by Kristen Proby
MASTER OF FREEDOM by Cherise Sinclair
CARESS OF PLEASURE by Julie Kenner
ADORED by Lexi Blake
HADES by Larissa Ione
RAVAGED by Elisabeth Naughton
DREAM OF YOU by Jennifer L. Armentrout
STRIPPED DOWN by Lorelei James
RAGE/KILLIAN by Alexandra Ivy/Laura Wright
DRAGON KING by Donna Grant
PURE WICKED by Shayla Black
HARD AS STEEL by Laura Kaye
STROKE OF MIDNIGHT by Lara Adrian
ALL HALLOWS EVE by Heather Graham
KISS THE FLAME by Christopher Rice
DARING HER LOVE by Melissa Foster
TEASED by Rebecca Zanetti
THE PROMISE OF SURRENDER by Liliana Hart

HALLOW BE THE HAUNT by Heather Graham
DIRTY FILTHY FIX by Laurelin Paige
THE BED MATE by Kendall Ryan
NIGHT GAMES by CD Reiss
NO RESERVATIONS by Kristen Proby
DAWN OF SURRENDER by Liliana Hart

COLLECTION FIVE
BLAZE ERUPTING by Rebecca Zanetti
ROUGH RIDE by Kristen Ashley
HAWKYN by Larissa Ione
RIDE DIRTY by Laura Kaye
ROME'S CHANCE by Joanna Wylde
THE MARRIAGE ARRANGEMENT by Jennifer Probst
SURRENDER by Elisabeth Naughton
INKED NIGHTS by Carrie Ann Ryan
ENVY by Rachel Van Dyken
PROTECTED by Lexi Blake
THE PRINCE by Jennifer L. Armentrout
PLEASE ME by J. Kenner
WOUND TIGHT by Lorelei James
STRONG by Kylie Scott
DRAGON NIGHT by Donna Grant
TEMPTING BROOKE by Kristen Proby
HAUNTED BE THE HOLIDAYS by Heather Graham
CONTROL by K. Bromberg
HUNKY HEARTBREAKER by Kendall Ryan
THE DARKEST CAPTIVE by Gena Showalter

COLLECTION SIX
DRAGON CLAIMED by Donna Grant
ASHES TO INK by Carrie Ann Ryan
ENSNARED by Elisabeth Naughton
EVERMORE by Corinne Michaels
VENGEANCE by Rebecca Zanetti
ELI'S TRIUMPH by Joanna Wylde
CIPHER by Larissa Ione
RESCUING MACIE by Susan Stoker
ENCHANTED by Lexi Blake

TAKE THE BRIDE by Carly Phillips
INDULGE ME by J. Kenner
THE KING by Jennifer L. Armentrout
QUIET MAN by Kristen Ashley
ABANDON by Rachel Van Dyken
THE OPEN DOOR by Laurelin Paige
CLOSER by Kylie Scott
SOMETHING JUST LIKE THIS by Jennifer Probst
BLOOD NIGHT by Heather Graham
TWIST OF FATE by Jill Shalvis
MORE THAN PLEASURE YOU by Shayla Black
WONDER WITH ME by Kristen Proby
THE DARKEST ASSASSIN by Gena Showalter

Discover Blue Box Press

TAME ME by J. Kenner
TEMPT ME by J. Kenner
DAMIEN by J. Kenner
TEASE ME by J. Kenner
REAPER by Larissa Ione
THE SURRENDER GATE by Christopher Rice
SERVICING THE TARGET by Cherise Sinclair

On Behalf of 1001 Dark Nights,

Liz Berry, M.J. Rose, and Jillian Stein would like to thank ~

Steve Berry
Doug Scofield
Benjamin Stein
Kim Guidroz
InkSlinger PR
Dan Slater
Asha Hossain
Chris Graham
Chelle Olson
Kasi Alexander
Jessica Johns
Dylan Stockton
Richard Blake
and Simon Lipskar

CPSIA information can be obtained
at www.ICGtesting.com
Printed in the USA
LVHW090454111220
673904LV00029B/204